Roseville Public Library
W9-CCP-559
Roseville, CA
NOV 2016
Roseville Public Library
3 1 2 7 1 0 0 6 7 2 8 9 5 0

blue
rider
press

PRETTY PAPER

ALSO BY WILLIE NELSON

It's a Long Story: My Life
(with David Ritz)

Roll Me Up and Smoke Me When I Die: Musings from the Road

A Tale Out of Luck: A Novel
(with Mike Blakely)

The Tao of Willie: A Guide to the Happiness in Your Heart
(with Turk Pipkin)

The Facts of Life: and Other Dirty Jokes

Willie: An Autobiography
(with Bud Shrake)

WILLIE
NELSON

PRETTY PAPER

A CHRISTMAS TALE

WILLIE NELSON

WITH DAVID RITZ

BLUE RIDER PRESS

NEW YORK

blue
rider
press

An imprint of Penguin Random House LLC
375 Hudson Street
New York, New York 10014

Library of Congress Cataloging-in-Publication Data

Names: Nelson, Willie, author. | Ritz, David, author.
Title: Pretty paper / Willie Nelson with David Ritz.
Description: New York : Blue Rider Press, 2016.
Identifiers: LCCN 2016029220 | ISBN 9780735211544 (hardcover)
Subjects: LCSH: Christmas stories. | BISAC: MUSIC / Genres & Styles / Country & Bluegrass. | RELIGION / Holidays / Christmas & Advent. | GSAFD: Autobiographical fiction.
Classification: LCC PS3614.E44957 P74 2016 | DDC 813/.6—dc23
LC record available at https://lccn.loc.gov/2016029220
p. cm.

Printed in the United States of America
1 3 5 7 9 10 8 6 4 2

Book design by Gretchen Achilles
Illustrations by Matthew Broughton

Pretty paper, pretty ribbons of blue,

Wrap your presents to your darling from you,

Pretty pencils to write "I love you,"

Pretty paper, pretty ribbons of blue.

Crowded street, busy feet hustle by him,

Downtown shoppers, Christmas is nigh.

There he sits all alone on the sidewalk,

Hoping that you won't pass him by.

Should you stop? Better not, much too busy,

You're in a hurry—my, how time does fly.

In the distance the ringing of laughter

And in the midst of the laughter he cries,

Pretty paper, pretty ribbons of blue,

Wrap your presents to your darling from you,

Pretty pencils to write "I love you,"

Pretty paper, pretty ribbons of blue.

CONTENTS

PRETTY PAPER

HAPPY HOLIDAYS

It was a rough Christmas in a rough town. Back in the early 1960s, Fort Worth was still the Wild West. There was no shortage of honky-tonks. The city was a haven for hustlers who'd mastered the art of living outside the law. Gangsters controlled the bookie joints, the brothels and most of the nightspots. In the midst of all this, I was struggling to get my career off the ground. Actually "career" is too fancy a word. I was a just a broke-ass picker looking to make a living making music. Running every which way—haunting the beer joints that hid in the shadows of the stockyards, soliciting the club owners who ran the buckets of blood out on Jacksboro Highway—I was getting nowhere fast. I did manage to get a gig deejaying on

KCNC, but that didn't last. Neither did my half-baked attempts to peddle Kirby vacuum cleaners and *Encyclopedia Americanas*. Proud to say, I was no good at convincing people—especially hardworking people—to buy stuff they didn't need. What I needed was a break.

And a break meant a hit song. I didn't care if I sang it or someone else did. If I found a bandleader who liked what I'd written, I'd sell my tune for the price of dinner. That's how desperate I was. Yet in the midst of my desperation, I also saw that others were more desperate than me. Which is where this story begins.

A week before Christmas, I was determined to get into the holiday spirit. Wasn't easy because my wife was singing the blues about bills we couldn't pay. We were living in a cramped two-room apartment with our three little ones. Most nights I was gone, looking for places to play my music, and by the time I got home, the kids were up and my wife was off to her waitress job. On this particular morning, two days before Christmas, my mother-in-law was good enough to watch the children while I drove downtown for some last-minute shopping. But, as luck would have it, my beat-up Ford Fairlane wouldn't start, the battery dead as a doornail. So I caught the bus.

I was freezing. The heater on the bus was busted, and my plaid wool jacket, which had seen better days, couldn't keep me warm. But what the hell. I was happy because last night I'd found a barroom—Big Bill's on Main Street near the slaughterhouses—where I could sing some of my songs. Folks liked what they heard and I wound up with twenty-five dollars' worth of tips in my pocket, a minor miracle. It was just the sort of encouragement that I needed to keep going. So today I wasn't bothered by the gray sky. Last night's tips told me that beyond the gray, the sun was shining. Besides, cold can be exhilarating. Best of all, snow was in the forecast, meaning that my kids might get to enjoy their first white Christmas.

I got off at Houston Street in the middle of downtown. The sidewalks were crowded with shoppers, men in fedoras and long overcoats, women in furs, kids bundled up with scarves and mittens. The store windows were decorated with wreaths and poinsettias. I could see my breath in the frosty air. Already a few flakes had begun to fall. Everyone's expectations were high. Everyone's heart was full. A beautiful Christmas was just around the corner—a Christmas when, at least for a day, we could forget our troubles and enjoy simple fellowship with family and friends.

Up ahead was Leonards, the mammoth department store that took up six city blocks, the establishment that advertised ONE-STOP SHOPPING WITH MORE MERCHANDISE FOR LESS MONEY. During the holidays, Leonards was also famous for installing a Santa Claus monorail and an elaborate Toyland department. When it came to Christmas cheer, Leonards was the spot.

But then, all of a sudden, a few steps down from the store's main entrance, I saw someone who stopped me in my tracks: a man, whose legs had been amputated above his knees, supporting himself on a large wooden board resting on four wheels. The board held not only the man but an array of neatly arranged products that he was selling—wrapping paper, pencils and ribbons. In addition to the traditional Christmas colors of green and red, his merchandise also came in blue, orange, purple and yellow. He easily moved around the board, supporting himself with his long, strong arms.

"Pretty paper!" he sang out in a strong and emotional voice. *"Pretty ribbons of blue . . . wrap your presents to your darling from you . . . pretty pencils to write 'I love you.'"*

He sang like he meant it. In fact, he sang like a singer. He sang in tune. Sadly, he also seemed to be singing in vain. I didn't see a single person stop to buy his wares. And yet that didn't stop his singing. I sensed that he sang to lift his spirits and stay warm. I stood about nine or ten feet away from him, off to one side, so he wouldn't see me studying him.

What I saw was a man who looked to be roughly my age—in his early thirties—a handsome man with chestnut-brown eyes and a brown beard covering his square-jawed face. He had a broad nose and thick eyebrows. He wore a black turtleneck sweater with big gaping holes. His blue jeans, which covered the stumps of his legs, were tattered. Despite his handicap, he projected a sense of confidence and rugged masculinity. As he sang his song peddling his wares, his eyes looked upward—above the crowds passing by, above Leonards department store, above the streetlights—into a sky filled with snowflakes growing fluffier by the minute. Some of the flakes landed on the man's eyes, melting on his lids and giving the impression that he was crying.

Was he crying? Was he distraught that no one found the time to stop and inquire about him or his colorful merchandise? I wanted to stop. I wanted to ask how he came to be doing what he was doing. How had he lost his legs? His deep brown eyes, wet with snow, suggested some story. But like the others, I did not stop. The Christmas rush was on, and even though I was in no rush at all, I picked up the rhythm of the downtown shoppers. I hurried along. I left the man on the rolling wooden board and rushed into the store.

I bought perfume for my wife, candy for my mother-in-law, a model train for my son and dolls for my girls. When the salesclerk asked if I wanted them gift-wrapped, without thinking I said, "Yes, please." But then I changed my mind. I thought of the man selling pretty paper. I wasn't much of a wrapper, but I could figure it out. This guy deserved a break, and buying his goods seemed like the right thing to do. After all, it was Christmas.

So with my unwrapped gifts, I left Leonards. Now the snow was coming down hard—a rare event in this part of Texas. The wind was kicking up a storm. The temperature had dipped down into single digits. It was hard to see, hard to walk against the howling wind. Folks were hanging on to light poles and the sides of buildings. Looking around, I couldn't see my man. Where had he gone? Maybe he'd moved on. Battling the wind, I circled all the way around Leonards enormous complex. I went up and down the block two, three, four times. Something told me I had to find him. But by now I was walking through a virtual blizzard.

I couldn't look forever. He'd probably found shelter in some nearby coffee shop. Or maybe he actually went inside Leonards to wait out the storm. So I reentered the store, where, for the next twenty minutes, I looked from one end to the other. But he was nowhere to be found. I gave up the search. Feeling a little guilty, I went to the clerks who had sold me my gifts and asked that they be wrapped. I was instructed to go to the third-floor gift-wrap department. After waiting in line for twenty minutes, I asked the gift wrapper—a hefty middle-aged woman wearing a Santa's cap—if she knew about the man who sold pretty paper, pencils and ribbons on the street outside the store.

"Oh, that bum," she said condescendingly. "He's nothing but a nuisance."

"He didn't seem like a bum," I said. "He sounded like a singer."

Busy making bows on the packages containing my daughters' dolls, the wrapper didn't respond. I'm not sure she heard what I said or, if she had, she didn't think it was worth a reply.

I took the presents and, still looking for the man as I headed for the exit, left Leonards. Outside, the weather had worsened. With a shopping bag in each hand, I was barely able to fight my way through the wind to the bus stop. Still no peddler in sight. Fortunately the bus came along in a few minutes—this one was heated—and I took my seat and rode back home.

We had a nice Christmas. Big Bill's made the difference. I worked there consistently through the holidays, meaning I could pay off some back bills and make peace—not to mention a little love—with my old lady. The kids loved their presents, my mother-in-law loved her chocolates, and I thought if I could keep gigging and save a little money, maybe, just maybe, I could make that move to Nashville, where I might have better luck selling my songs.

FOLLOWING A DREAM

A couple of weeks had passed and I'd nearly forgotten all about the man selling his wares in front of Leonards when all of a sudden he turned up in a dream. Now, I'm not one who remembers my dreams, and if I do, I don't pay them much mind. But this dream was different. This dream was incredibly vivid. The peddler showed up in living color, and he was playing guitar, and he was standing tall. His legs were long and sturdy and he was singing a song. I can't remember the words or melody. But I was sure it was the most beautiful song I had ever heard. He said that the song was the story of his life. At one point in the dream, I was standing right next to him in the band, playing my guitar, and at another point I was in the audience cheering him on. When the song was over, I went over to congratulate him, but he had disappeared. I tried to find him but he was long gone. I was out there on some lonely highway, looking every which way for this man. I had to know his name. I had to hear this song again, but there was nothing but the cold starless night and the sound of howling coyotes. I woke up feeling the same frustration I felt when I went looking for him the first time outside of Leonards.

I tried to forget the dream but couldn't. Had my morning coffee. Drove the kids to school. Came back to the house. Made a few calls about possible gigs. Drank more coffee. Smoked a cigarette. Read the paper. Downed another cup of coffee. But no matter what I did, the dream wouldn't leave me. So I picked up my guitar to see if I could re-create that haunting melody I had heard in my sleep. I couldn't. I couldn't salvage the song. I heard only fragments. The more I tried to reconstruct the dream, the further it floated away from me. That's when I decided to go back to Leonards to see if the guy was still there.

My old Fairlane was on its last legs but, coughing and belching, somehow made it downtown. With the holidays over, I was worried that the peddler had moved on. I wasn't sure why I was taking the time to look for him. Hustling my music—that's what I needed to do. The gig at Big Bill's was still on, but the place was feeling the effects of the post-holiday doldrums. Come January, folks were partied out. Half of me was hoping that the legless man wouldn't be there. That way I could just put him out of my mind. But the other half—the half that probably speaks for my conscience—was pushing me on. Can't explain why I needed to see him. All I can tell you is that I did.

He was there.

He was in the exact same spot where I'd seen him last time. He was there on his wooden board, wearing the same tattered sweater and jeans, crying out with those same singsong words about his pretty paper, pencils and ribbons. Unlike last time, though, the street was not crowded with shoppers. A few women, a few kids, a few businessmen, but nobody taking note of him. Nobody giving him the time of day.

I parked across the street and walked over to greet him.

"Hey, man," I said, "last time I came looking for you it seemed like you were blown away in a blizzard."

"Why were you looking for me?" he asked in a Texas accent that echoed my own.

"Needed some of those wrapping papers and ribbons."

"Well, you found me now."

"To tell you the truth, I don't need 'em anymore."

The man didn't say anything. Didn't register disappointment. Didn't blink. Stoic as a stone.

"Just wanted to introduce myself," I said, extending my hand. "I'm Willie."

He took my hand and shook it. Strong grip.

"Vernon. Vernon Clay."

"Nice meeting you, Vernon. You from around here?"

"Not far."

Vernon Clay wasn't exactly interested in striking up a conversation. He averted his eyes and, using his arms to turn his body away from me, started arranging his papers and pencils.

I wasn't sure what to say. I could simply tell him the truth—that I was curious about who he was and how he got here. But somehow those words didn't come out. Instead I said something stupid. I said, "Tough way to make a living."

Vernon turned back toward me. His eyes were hard. His eyes said what I already knew: *Dumb comment. Obvious comment. Insensitive comment.*

Trying to recover, I said, "I mean, I hear you singing and figured you for a musician."

Several seconds passed before Vernon said, "You figured right."

"Me too," I said. "I'm a picker. And a songwriter. And something of a singer."

"Good for you."

I could understand his sarcasm. He just wanted to be left alone to sell his wares. Part of me thought it best to leave him alone. But that other part of me that got me here—the curious part—made me stand my ground. Several awkward seconds of silence passed.

Vernon finally said, "Look, mister—"

"Willie," I corrected him.

"Okay, Willie. If you're a songwriter, you need pencils."

"I do. Fact is, I'm clean out of pencils. I'll buy a half dozen."

"That'll be a buck fifty."

I gave him two bucks.

"Keep the change."

"Thanks."

He handed me six pencils. Transaction complete. Now that I was a paying customer, I figured I had the right to ask him a couple of more questions. But right about then, a talkative woman in a wide-brimmed cardinal-red hat came up to him and started asking about his wrapping paper and ribbons. He turned his attention to her. I didn't want to be a nuisance, so I took my pencils and went home.

I felt a little frustrated. I hadn't learned a damn thing about him. But being a private person myself, who was I to pry into this guy's life? He had a certain pride that should be respected. And that was that.

Except it wasn't.

BACK TO BIG BILL'S

By early February, business had picked up at Big Bill's. I'd put together a little band and built up enough of a following to where I could work five nights a week. I was also coming up with a few ideas for new songs. I'm one of those writers who can't force it. Like babies, songs come down the chute when they're good and ready. Unlike children, though, songs don't have a gestation period you can roughly measure. Some songs take years to come alive. Those are the years when your unconscious mind is doing the work. You gotta be patient. I learned that early on.

But this one song I called "Pretty Paper" found its way into the world damn fast. Naturally it was based on seeing Vernon Clay that snowy day in December. That convinced me that the emotions I was feeling for him—whether it was curiosity or sympathy—were real. The mystery surrounding the man really intrigued me. Of course, the song didn't answer any questions or give a clue to his story—because I really didn't know his story. The song merely set the scene that was still so vivid in my mind. I guess my reasoning was that now that the song was written, I didn't have to solve his mystery. He could remain a question mark, a man frozen in time whose past, present and future would always be unknown.

And then—wouldn't you know it—he reappeared out of nowhere.

Well, not exactly nowhere. Big Bill's is definitely somewhere. It's a rough-and-tumble barroom uncomfortably close to the slaughterhouses. I say "uncomfortably" because if the wind's blowing in a certain direction, the air ain't exactly perfumed. There's no sign outside, just a neon replica of a bottle of Pearl beer. There didn't need to be any sign 'cause everyone in the neighborhood knows Big Bill. For years he worked on the kill floors where the cattle are slaughtered. That's where he got into a fight with one of his bosses, who Big Bill caught shortchanging him. He slit the man's throat. The man survived and Bill served six years for attempted murder. Once out, he was recruited by Nathan "Nutsy" Perkins, a well-known gangster, as an enforcer. At six-foot-six and three hundred pounds, Bill was good at his job. But he soon tired of doing Nutsy's dirty work and quit. This was unusual. No one quits Nutsy, at least no one who values his life. But as testimony to Bill's menacing stature, Nutsy let him walk away. Fact is, Nutsy owned the building where Bill put his bar. Rumor was, Nutsy was so anxious to stay cool with Bill that he didn't even charge him rent.

From time to time, you'd see Nutsy and some of his boys at the bar. Nutsy was a talker. Had an opinion about everything, especially the local politicians. He liked to brag how most of them were in his pocket. He'd come to Fort Worth from Chicago as a teenager and never lost that Midwestern nasal twang. He had a lanky frame, a long nose, dark thinning hair and alert eyes the color of dark chocolate. He usually wore a white fedora with a purple feather on the brim. No Western getup for Nutsy. He went for pin-striped suits, white shirts and white silk ties. He also had no taste for music. Didn't matter who was on the bandstand, Nutsy never shut up. Unless Big Bill told him to.

Because Big Bill liked music. He respected musicians. I first won him over when I played "Blue Christmas." He especially appreciated that I sang Ernest

Tubb's version, not Elvis's. Towering over everyone as he stood behind the bar, Bill was serving up drinks when, hearing the song, he cracked a broken-tooth smile that lit up his scarred face. When I sang Tubb's "Waltz Across Texas," I saw tears in his eyes. "Mama and Daddy used to dance to that ol' tune," he told me later that night—the same December night he hired me to play weekends.

Big Bill also prided himself on maintaining the best jukebox in the city. Of course there were the current hits of Porter Wagoner, George Jones, Buck Owens and Patsy Cline, but Bill also loaded it up with his favorite singers from a bygone era—Eddy Arnold, Lefty Frizzell, Hank Thompson and of course Hank Williams and his Drifting Cowboys. Every night around closing time, Bill would walk over to the jukebox, and while he cleaned up, he'd play Williams's "Lovesick Blues" four times in a row.

The crowd at Big Bill's could get rowdy. It was a place where men came looking for women and women—some of them pros—were just as rowdy as the men. You'd see an occasional fistfight or knife fight, but, because of Big Bill's reputation as an enforcer, you wouldn't have to worry about shootings. The bandstand—rickety old wooden planks—ran across the back wall to where I could see who was coming in and heading out. There were no tables or chairs. You either drank at the long bar or just stood around. Dancers tended to dance right in front of the bandstand. If the music was right, though, folks would be dancing all over the place. The sign said it was unlawful to have more than eighty people in there, but on a good Saturday night, at least twice that number of party people were packed in like sardines.

It was on such a Saturday night—a chilly night in late February—when I was feeling especially good. I'd finally found a drummer who understood my personal sense of rhythm. Not everyone does. But Brother Paul, a Fort Worth native, did. If I ran a little ahead or lagged a little behind, Paul followed me. He sensed where I wanted to go. He was also at home at a joint like Big Bill's. He was friends with Bill and had done business with Nutsy Perkins. Paul knew his way around the underside of the city. In his wide-brimmed black hat, his red-lined black cape and his shitkicker boots, he made a statement: *I am here, and I've got your back.* He also packed heat, and wasn't shy about letting shady promoters know it. Brother Paul turned out to be a rock-solid bandmate and protective friend.

On that particular night I didn't need protection. There was a warm feeling all around. Big Bill was happy that I played a few of his favorites by Bob Wills and Gene Autry. The crowd seemed to like my rendition of hits by Johnny Cash and Marty Robbins like "Ring of Fire" and "El Paso." I snuck in a couple of my originals that went over pretty good. In between numbers, I could hear Nutsy Perkins yakking at the bar, but when I started singing I also saw Big Bill give him the high sign to shut up. Only Big Bill had the balls to do that.

If I'm to be honest—and I always try to be—I had my eye on a little lady that looked like she had her eye on me. She'd been coming to Bill's nearly every Saturday since I started there. My marriage was going through a bumpy stage and I guess you could say that I was easily tempted. Hell, bumpy stage or not, I've always been easily tempted. This gal stood about five-foot-five, with long black hair, flashing dark eyes and curves in all the right places. Sometimes she came in with a man, and sometimes she came in alone. To-night she was alone. Right in front of the bandstand, she even danced alone, swaying back and forth to the songs I was singing. As she swayed, she kept her eyes on me, and quite naturally I offered her a big smile.

I found this flirtation so exciting that I ended the set early in order to make her acquaintance. Turned out her name was Barbara Lou. She worked as a beau-tician in Arlington and had aspirations of becoming a singer. She told me she also wrote songs. I said I'd love to hear them.

"Oh, they're not nearly as good as yours," she said. "They're silly ideas. Just little poems."

"Far as songs go," I said, "the simpler the better. A lot of songs began as poems. Let me hear one of yours."

"Right here?"

"Why not?"

"They're all about love," she said.

"Well, the world can always use another love song."

"Might be easier to let you hear one if there weren't so many people around."

"How 'bout after the show?" I suggested.

"Well, maybe," she said, with what seemed like in-sincere hesitancy.

"I got one more set. Any requests?"

"Something you wrote."

"I was actually thinking about singing something I wrote around Christmastime. It's a different kind of song for me."

"A holiday song?"

"A moody holiday song. Little bit of a sad holiday song."

"Well, I'd love to hear it."

That's all the encouragement I needed to sing "Pretty Paper" in public for the first time. I'd gone over it with my bass player and Brother Paul a few days earlier. It was an easy song to play. I figured it was good to end a long night on a calm, thoughtful note.

The last set started with a couple of up-tempo tunes. The place had thinned out a bit, but there were folks who still wanted to dance. I slowed it down for all the hopeful guys who needed cheek-to-cheek time to make their final plea. Then, after a couple of ballads, I got ready to sing "Pretty Paper." I'm not one to talk much on the bandstand. I hardly ever introduce songs. I learned that as a kid watching Bob Wills. Folks don't come to hear you talk. They come to hear you play.

Singing "Pretty Paper" for the first time in public gave me a real eerie feeling. On that Saturday night—actually it was nearly three a.m. on Sunday morning—I felt a chill pass over me. The chill seemed to affect everyone. As I sang, the room froze. Dancers stopped dancing. People stopped talking. Even Nutsy clammed up. Behind the bar, Big Bill stood still as a statue. Maybe it was my imagination, but I got the idea everyone was fixated on the story I was singing.

"*Pretty paper,*" I sang, "*pretty ribbons of blue . . . Crowded street, busy feet hustle by him . . . Downtown shoppers, Christmas is nigh . . . There he sits all alone on the sidewalk . . . Hoping that you won't pass him by . . . Should you stop? Better not, much too busy . . . You're in a hurry—my, how time does fly . . . In the distance the ringing of laughter . . . And in the midst of the laughter he cries . . . 'Pretty paper, pretty ribbons of blue.'*"

When I got through, I had a lump in my throat. I saw that Barbara Lou had a tear in her eye.

"That's it, folks," I said. "Thanks for coming out. Be careful getting home, and see ya next time."

My initial idea was to make a beeline for Barbara Lou and see exactly what she had in mind. But as I walked off the bandstand, she had melted into the crowd. Hoping she hadn't already left, I looked outside. That's when I saw Vernon—the same Vernon Clay I'd seen at Leonards—roll by on his board. Could be no mistake. It was definitely Vernon. Had he been in the club when I sang the song, and I just hadn't seen him? Did the song piss him off and did he take off in a hurry? Or was he just passing by and hadn't heard me at all? One way or the other, I had to know. I had to catch him.

I quickly made my way to the door, but before I could get there, a bear of a man grabbed me by my arm.

"You been chasing after my woman," he said in a voice that let me know he was out-of-his-mind drunk.

I saw his eyes were raging red. I also saw a switchblade in his right hand. Standing next to him was sweet Barbara Lou. She just shrugged her shoulders, as if to say, "I didn't know this would happen."

What happened next was that the switchblade sprang open. Then the man sprang for my throat. It all happened in an instant. With no time to react, I saw my life flash before me. But fate interceded. A split second before the blade reached my skin, an empty bottle of Lone Star beer came crashing down on my assailant's head. The man crumbled to the floor. I wasn't scratched. Standing over the guy with a broken bottle in his hand was my drummer, Brother Paul. Not missing a beat, Paul stomped on the man's hand. The blade went flying across the floor and stopped at the bar stool where Nutsy Perkins was sitting.

"Your drummer's good," said Nutsy. "He's right on time."

"Throw the bum outta here," Big Bill ordered.

Brother Paul picked up the man, who was half-conscious, and flung him on the sidewalk. In all the confusion, Barbara Lou had managed to disappear and, even more disturbing, so had Vernon.

SUNDAY SCHOOL

I was raised up in a Methodist church in the small town of Abbott, Texas. I've never had reason to doubt the lessons I learned there. I was told that a Perfect Man came to earth to teach us a couple of basics—love everyone and help those in need. I've tried to follow that code but, as an imperfect man, I haven't always succeeded. During my Fort Worth years, struggling to make my way in this world, I felt moved to reconnect with my roots. So I volunteered to teach Sunday school. I liked reading the Bible stories and discussing them with kids. That meant I had to keep things simple, which is how I like it.

Not all the church elders were keen on having a picker teach the young ones. But the senior pastor was a good man who saw I was sincere. He signed me up, and every Sunday I arrived with Bible in hand. Many were the times I left the barroom at three a.m., went home to grab few hours of sleep before showering, putting on my suit and heading to church.

After the incident at Big Bill's, we had a week of dangerous weather. A twister had ripped through the city, destroying a trailer park and killing three people. The building where Bill housed his bar was badly damaged and closed up for repairs. All week long I thought about going back to Leonards to see if Vernon was there, but the storms stopped me. I wondered how the storms affected Vernon. The man was still on my mind.

By Sunday, the weather broke and the sun came out strong and unseasonably warm. The air was crisp and clean. Because I hadn't worked Saturday night, I got a good night's rest. I arrived at Sunday school early. Before I even began discussing that morning's lesson, Danny, a ten-year-old, raised his hand and said, "I saw on the television how that big tornado killed some people."

"I saw that too," I said. "Terrible thing."

"Were those bad people who died?"

"Wouldn't think so. I have no reason to believe so."

"Well, if God is good, why did God let it happen?"

"Wasn't God who did it. It was nature."

"But isn't God in charge of nature? Isn't He in charge of everything?"

Danny was bringing up a serious issue, and I had to pause. I owed him a truthful answer.

"The truth is that we don't understand everything about God. Our minds aren't that big. But I can tell you this for sure—when we let God take charge of our hearts, we always do the right thing."

"How can you tell it's the right thing?" asked Danny.

"It's like when you share your food with someone who's real hungry. It feels good. Feels good on the inside."

"My granddaddy busted his hip and can't walk too good. So I helped him down the porch steps this morning. Is that what you mean?"

Smiling, I said, "That's just what I mean."

For the rest of the morning, I abandoned the planned lesson and let the kids tell stories of how they had helped out others—and how good it felt. Freckle-faced Mary talked about directing a fireman to the family cat caught up in the tree. Manuel proudly explained how he helped teach the alphabet to his younger brother. Paulette told us how she watched television with her blind aunt and described everything that was on the screen. Last Thanksgiving, Tommy joined his mom at the food bank serving turkey dinner to destitute families.

When everyone had a chance to talk about their good deed, Danny pointed to me and said, "Your turn."

I had to stop and think. What had I done? Vernon Clay came to mind. I wanted to cite him as example, but what could I say? He was simply someone I had written a song about. I couldn't say I'd helped him, because I hadn't.

"I'm working on a good cause," I said, "and you all have inspired me to keep at it."

After church I went out of my way to drive past Leonards. Vernon wasn't there. In those days, department stores were closed Sundays and downtown was deserted. But I was back Monday afternoon, and sure enough, he was at his usual spot. He was still selling pencils, but in place of holiday wrapping paper he had a stack of school supplies—spiral notebooks, yellow pads and crayons. He had replaced the tattered sweater with a worn red-checked flannel shirt. He still wore the same jeans cut off where his legs ended above what would have been his knees. His singsong cry had also changed from "pretty paper" to "pencils, pads and crayons."

"Hey, Vernon," I said as I extended my hand. He took it and shook it forcefully. "Didn't I see you outside Big Bill's a couple of Saturday nights ago?"

His eyes regarded me quickly and then turned away.

"Don't know who you saw," he said indifferently.

"Well, it was definitely you. Wasn't sure whether you'd been inside or were just passing through."

"What difference would that make to you?"

"I was performing that night. I was singing with my little band, and I was wondering if you got to hear us."

"Didn't hear nothing. These days I don't go out of my way to hear music."

"That's a shame."

"That's just a fact."

"Music lifts our spirits. That's the whole point of music, isn't it?"

Looking away from me, Vernon didn't say a word.

Looking to fill in the long silence, I said, "Didn't you say you were once a singer?"

"I didn't say anything. You here to buy something or ask a bunch of questions?"

I understood Vernon's hostility. I was a busybody, invading the man's privacy. At this point I had to figure out once and for all what it was I was doing there. What did I want from this guy?

I finally said it plain: "To tell you the truth, man, I'm just damn curious about you."

"You ain't the first," he shot back.

"And I suspect I won't be the last."

"And what does all this curiosity get me?"

I didn't have a ready answer. I had to think about it. A few seconds later I gave what I thought to be a reasonable answer.

"A chance to tell your story," I said.

For the first time Vernon focused his eyes directly on me. His eyes were filled with suspicion.

"There's nothing in it for me," he said.

"There's a chance for you to unburden yourself."

"Who says I'm burdened?" he snapped.

I took a chance and said, "I do. It's something I feel in your spirit."

"Oh, so now you're some kind of mystical reader of spirits."

"I didn't say that. I just said that I'm sensing something heavy that maybe could be lightened."

Rather than respond to me, he sang out his sales

song to a few people passing by. "Pencils! Pads! Pretty crayons!"

One lady, accompanied by identical twin girls, stopped to peruse the merchandise. She liked what she saw and so did the kids. They bought a bunch of stuff with a twenty-dollar bill and told Vernon to keep the change.

"Nice sale," I said. "Standing here, I must be bringing you good luck."

"Standing there you're blocking the sun."

"I'll move."

"Good. And keep moving."

Well, that was it. Vernon couldn't have been clearer. He had no interest in making a new friend, no interest in opening up, no need of me. The only polite thing to do was to leave the man alone. So I did.

"Sorry if I bothered you," I said. "Good luck."

I waited for him to extend his hand or at least look up and say good-bye. But he did neither.

CHILI RICE IS VERY NICE

A day later I drove over to Big Bill's. Felt the need, I suppose, to hang out with some people who, unlike Vernon, wouldn't mind seeing me.

Bill was busy supervising the installation of a large piece of glass for his front window, which had been blown out in the storm. After the repair had been made, he invited me in for a beer. On the jukebox, George Jones was singing "Tender Years."

"Once I fix that busted drainpipe in the back, I should be open for business tomorrow," he said. "Tuesday nights are slow, but if you and your boys wanna play for tips, have at it."

"Might be a good way to keep us out of trouble."

"Talking of trouble, the other night before that trouble broke out—before that jackass came at you with a knife—I was fixing to ask you about that song you sang, the one about Christmas shopping."

"'Pretty Paper'?"

"That's the one. You were writing about Vernon, weren't you? The guy with no legs who's always out there in front of Leonards."

"Yeah, he did inspire me. Fact is, I've been trying to talk to him and learn his story."

"Good luck," said Big Bill sarcastically. "He don't say nothing to no one. Been living down the street for nearly two years. Comes in once in a blue moon for a shot a whisky. I give it to him for free. But he don't say a word. I'm lucky if I get a 'thanks.'"

"When you say 'down the street,' where exactly do you mean?"

"You know Chester's Chili Rice?"

"I know where it is."

"Well, Chester and his wife, Essie, live upstairs, and they let Vernon stay in a shack out back. Don't ask me why."

Knowing it was pointless, I didn't ask Bill any more questions about Vernon. Instead I asked, "How's the chili rice over there at Chester's?"

"Never tasted better chili. Man, you gotta try it."

"Maybe I will."

Maybe it was a sign—me stopping in at Bill's to learn, without asking, where Vernon lived. Maybe the universe was trying to tell me something. Or maybe it was just a bunch of coincidences. Whatever it was, my curiosity was rearoused. And besides, I was hungry as hell. A big bowl of chili sounded good.

There was a long line outside the door of the narrow little store. Above the open door, the sign crudely carved out of rough wood simply said GOOD EATS. Nothing about Chester and his chili. I peeked inside and saw there were no tables, only a small counter running against the back wall that allowed seven or eight people to stand up and eat. No stools. Most everyone was ordering takeout. I was also interested to see that the crowd was mixed between white and black, something of an oddity for Texas in the early 1960s. An old brown Crosley Bakelite radio was blasting KNOK, the Fort Worth rhythm-and-blues station. Bobby "Blue" Bland's "Stormy Monday" felt like the right song at the right time. So did B.B. King's "How Blue Can You Get?" The blues was brewing, and so was a huge pot of chili, whose spicy fragrance was enough to make a ravenous man dizzy. Once inside, I looked around and saw that the walls were plastered with train schedules and punched-out train tickets. There had to be thousands of them. Made for fascinating wallpaper.

As I approached the counter, I studied the face of the black man taking orders. I presumed this was Chester. He looked to be in his sixties. His hair was sprinkled with gray and his eyes were an unusual shade of green. He stood over six feet and, although hefty, was not fat. His manner was calm. The big hungry crowd hardly threw him. He just kept taking orders and shouting 'em out to the woman behind him who was stirring a huge pot of chili and serving it up in cardboard cups. She was half his size, a petite lady with lightning-fast hands, whose concentration was fierce. Your choices were basic—a single or double. Most everyone was ordering doubles, so when I got to the head of the line and found myself face-to-face with Chester, I followed suit.

"A double, please."

"You probably want a lemonade to go with that."

"What else you have to drink?"

"That's it."

"Then lemonade it is."

"Extra-large?"

"Sure thing."

"For here or to go?"

"I'll eat it here. I like how you've decorated your place," I said, looking around. "You work for the railroad?"

"Forty years. Proud member of the Brotherhood of Sleeping Car Porters."

"Congratulations."

"Enjoy your food."

"Chili rice is very nice!" the lady at the stove suddenly cried out.

"Eat it once and you'll eat it twice!" several of the in-line customers yelled in response. I presumed this was a ritual.

I watched the woman prepare my order. She took a couple of dollops of chili and dropped 'em over a mountain of rice. Then she added chopped onions, a thick slab of butter and a rich red salsa. The final topping was a generous layer of freshly grated cheese. The double chili, plus the lemonade, was a buck and a quarter.

Big Bill was right. The dish was crazy good. So good, in fact, that I had to go back for a single.

"Liked it, huh?" asked Chester.

"You bet. Helluva recipe you got there."

"I know. It's a blessing how it came about."

"How did it come about?"

"Lemme wait on these customers behind you. The dinner rush will be over in a few minutes. Stick around and I'll tell you the story."

I stuck around. I even toyed with a second single but managed to restrain myself. The stuff was addictive. I enjoyed watching Chester and his cook working in perfect tandem. Harmony's a beautiful thing, and not just in music. The music from the old Crosley radio kept pouring out sounds that I found soothing. This was around the time that Ray Charles had released his country album, and they were playing it on all the stations, black and white. Who doesn't love Ray singing "I Can't Stop Loving You"?

Didn't have to wait more than a half hour before the place started emptying out. I went over and introduced myself to Chester.

"That's my wife, Essie," he said. "My wife and my sure-enough partner."

"Is she the lady I need to congratulate for this fabulous chili?" I asked.

"Can't take no credit for that," said Essie.

"She cooks it up better than anyone," said Chester. "But it wasn't her idea. Wasn't mine either. Came about in a strange way. You see, while I was working the trains all those years, Essie was working as a cook for the Zale family, the ones that own all those jewelry stores. Damn good cook, too. Her idea was to retire when I retired. Then we'd open a chicken and waffles restaurant. You see, we never had kids and, given how we're both tight with a dollar, we'd put some good money away. This is some five years back. Essie'd been cooking this fried chicken, mind you, her whole life. People swore by it. And the waffles were light and fluffy. We opened our place right in this here location, but for some reason, try as we might, we couldn't catch a fly in here. We put up flyers on the telephone poles, even gave away free samples in the barrooms, but we just didn't catch on.

"We were just about to close up shop when one day this man comes in—a white man without no legs. He moves along on a wooden board with wheels, using his arms. Got him these real powerful arms. You can't help but feel sorry for him, so I tell him don't worry about paying for his food. Naturally he's grateful. While he's eating his chicken, he overhears me and Essie talking about closing down. Very polite-like, he asks why would we do that when the food's so good. 'Probably 'cause there's so many other places where you can get fried chicken.' 'Have you ever thought about chili?' he asks. 'I like chili,' I say, 'but it's not one of Essie's specialties.' Then he proceeds to talk about this recipe his grandma used and he'd be happy to give it to us. Can't explain why, but something told me to listen to this man. Something about how downright genuine he was. So right then and there I ran out and bought all the ingredients he told me to get. Step by step, he told Essie what to do. A little bit of this, little bit of that, stir it, dice it, salt it, sweeten it—you know. I'm no cook, so I can't even tell how it came together."

"I can," said Essie. "I knew straight off that this man knew what he was talking about. When I whipped up the first batch, he tasted it and said, no, it wasn't exactly right. I'd oversalted. So I tried it again. Can you believe it took nine or ten times before it got the flavor he said was right."

"That's when I tasted it," said Chester. "And, man, that's when I was sold. No doubt. This chili rice was a winner."

"And the man who gave you the recipe is Vernon, the same man who sells pencils and paper?" I asked.

"Oh, you're a friend of Vernon's?" asked Chester.

"Didn't think Vernon had any friends," said Essie.

"Not exactly a friend," I said. "An acquaintance. Big Bill from down the street told me he lives here."

"That's the least we could do for Vernon," said Chester. "He wouldn't take no money, not a dime. Said as long as we let 'im eat that chili for free, that was enough."

"But it wasn't enough," said Essie. "Not when I followed him home one day to find out he had no home. Poor soul was living out by the railroad tracks in some nasty ol' toolshed. I said, 'Vernon, this will not do. Not after you helped us the way you did. We got a little one-room apartment back of this building we bought with our savings. We were thinking of renting it out, and it looks like we done found a tenant.' 'Can't afford it,' he said. That's when I put my foot down and said, 'Decision's been made, Vernon. God has blessed us by bringing you in our life, and all we are doing is giving back the blessing. You ain't charging us nothing for your recipe and we ain't charging you nothing for a decent place to stay.'"

"When did all this happen?" I asked.

"A year this past Christmas. Yes, sir, it all happened around Christmas. And then in January, this writer wrote up something nice in the newspaper about our chili rice and suddenly we went from going broke to landing in high cotton."

"Beautiful story," I said.

"Beautiful man," said Essie about Vernon.

"I tried to get him to talk about himself," I said, "but I didn't get anywhere."

Essie laughed. "When it comes to saying anything personal-like, he clams up. I learned that right away. You can't help but be curious about what happened to him, but out of respect I stopped asking. Cannot for the life of me, though, understand how a human soul can live without the comfort of some company, at least every once in a while."

"I got the idea he'd been a musician," I said.

"What makes you think so?" asked Essie.

"Being a musician myself, ma'am, I heard the way he sang out when he was selling his paper and pencils."

"I thought the same thing myself," said Chester. "He don't say much, but when he do, you can hear music in what he's saying. One time I thought I heard guitar music coming from his room out back. Sounded mighty pretty, too. Be good if he had him a musician friend. Someone to bring out the music in him."

"I'd like to talk to him about that."

"You know what," Essie said decisively, "I'm gonna tell him that. No, I'm gonna do more than tell him. I'm gonna bring you back there and let him know what I think."

"He's home?"

"He came in a few hours ago. Lord knows what he's up to all alone. 'Bout time he had him a friend."

"Now, Essie," cautioned Chester, "you best leave well enough alone."

"I can tell this man standing in front of me has a good heart," Essie answered. "Besides, somewhere in the Good Book, it says to do for others what they can't do for themselves. This here is one of those times."

A STELLA HARMONY

Taking charge, Essie led me around back. She knocked on the door of a freestanding building no bigger than a two-car garage.

"Who is it?" asked a deep voice from within.

"Essie."

The door opened immediately. I looked down at Vernon and Vernon looked up at me. He was standing on the stumps of his legs. And clearly not happy to see me. But before he could complain, Essie chimed in.

"He's a musician," she said, referring to me, "and him and me were both guessing that somewhere in your soul there's music waiting to come out."

As she said that, I spotted a Stella Harmony guitar leaning against a mattress in the back of the room.

"Hey, I got one of those," I said, pointing to the instrument. "Was my first. Fresh out of the Sears catalogue. Wouldn't part with it for the world."

"There are a lot of Stella guitars around," said Vernon.

"Those damn things are indestructible," I said. "They mellow with age."

"Well, while you boys go on talking about guitars," said Essie, "I've got a kitchen to clean up." And with that, she was gone.

"So you managed to chase me down," said Vernon.

"Chalk it up to coincidence," I said. "I was over at Big Bill's, who mentioned that you live here. Then the chili rice called to me. Blame it on the chili rice. Chester and Essie say you're the man behind its magic."

"No magic," he said. "Just an old recipe."

"They said it was Grandma's."

"Yup, she was the woman who raised me."

"Funny," I said. "I was raised by my grandmother. Where was your mom?"

"Where was yours?" he asked.

"Sowing her wild oats. Not ready to raise kids."

Vernon nodded his head. I waited to hear about his mom, but he wasn't talking. As he turned his back to me, I had a few seconds to look around his apartment. The setup was simple. Not far from the door, a low-to-the-floor armchair faced a battered Emerson television set. Behind the TV was a long table that held his supply of papers, pencils, ribbons and notepads, all neatly arranged. Next to the table was his four-wheeled board. On one side of the room was a small stepladder, a sink and stovetop. Over the stovetop was a cabinet and, just beyond that, a door that I presumed led to a bathroom. Although sparse, the place was spotless—no dust, no dirty dishes in the sink.

With his arms, Vernon lifted his body off the ground and, in a series of short quick maneuvers, propelled himself to the back of the room where his guitar was resting. He picked it up and started to strum. I took that as the first positive sign he'd given me since I first set eyes on him in front of Leonards. As he played, though, his eyes weren't on me. His eyes were far off in the distance.

From the first few notes, I could hear that he was

a serious guitarist. He wasn't playing any particular song, just a slow-moving deep-feeling blues. But unlike a lot of blues guitarists who fall on clichés, Vernon chose his notes carefully and creatively. His phrasing came from his heart, not his head. I heard him crying through his music.

"Where'd you learn to play like that?" I asked.

"I had a teacher when I was a kid."

"He ever record?"

"Nope. He'd say to me, 'For every Robert Johnson and Django Reinhardt, there are a dozen guys just as good that you never heard of. Well, Vernon, I'm one of 'em.'"

Saying that, Vernon, for the first time in my presence, broke into a small smile. The smile, though, didn't last long. Focused on the guitar, he dug deeper into his blues.

"What was your teacher's name?" I asked.

"Skeeter. Skeeter Jarvis."

"He still around?"

"Died years ago."

"Looks like he did a helluva job with you. Whatever he taught seems to have stuck."

"Compared to him, I ain't shit. Skeeter could play the thing over his head, behind his back, even with his teeth. Played it right-handed or left-handed, didn't make him no difference. He liked to say that he played so pretty, women would leave their husband's bed in the middle of the night, just to hear him."

"Sounds like a song," I said.

"He lived his life like a song."

"A black man, I presume."

"No. White man. But he said he'd learned to play from black men like Lightnin' Hopkins and Mance Lipscomb. His main man was Bukka 'Bottleneck' Dupree. Skeeter told me a story about Bottleneck I'll never forget. One day when Bottleneck was showing Skeeter how to work the slide, a friend of Bottleneck's passed by and said, 'You're wasting your time. That white boy ain't ever gonna get it.' 'If you don't think white boys get the blues,' Bottleneck shouted, 'you're as stupid as you look!' To prove his point, a couple of months later Bottleneck put Skeeter in his little band that played in roadhouses for blacks only. But Skeeter didn't stay long 'cause it turned out he was afraid of playing in front of big crowds. That was his downfall, the reason he never made it big."

"But Skeeter could really play the blues."

"The man could play anything—Western swing, jazz, you name it. But the blues, he said, was the truth."

"And that's how this whole music thing started for you?" I asked.

Rather than answer my question, Vernon went back to playing, his head hanging down over the guitar, his eyes shut. He played a little Robert Johnson, a little Lightnin' Hopkins, a little Leadbelly. He played a snippet of a Mance Lipscomb song called "Mother Had a Sick Child." He played Elmore James's "Dust My Broom."

"What about Hank Williams?" I asked. "You must have grown up on Hank."

"Skeeter claimed to have played with Hank. Said they both came up in Alabama. Skeeter swore that Hank wanted to make him one of the Drifting Cowboys, but a woman got in the way. Apparently him and Hank were after the same lady. You should have heard Skeeter sing 'Lovesick Blues.' I love to sing it myself."

I've heard "Lovesick Blues" a thousand times. Hank owned that song. His version is a thing of beauty. But hearing Vernon do it, I have to confess that I forgot about Hank. Vernon reinvented it. He put so much of himself in his singing that I, a guy who doesn't cry easily, felt myself tearing up. Inside his voice I heard a lifetime of hurt. God only knows what this man had gone through to sound this way. There had to be an epic story behind his suffering.

When he was through, all I could say was "That was really something."

Vernon didn't say a word. His eyes were still shut. His guitar remained cradled in his arms. No motion at all. I let a few seconds tick by and then said, "With a voice as good as yours, I can't believe you never made a record."

"Who said I never made a record?" he said, now opening his eyes and staring right at me.

"I presumed . . ."

"You presumed wrong."

"Tell me about it. You have a copy for me to hear?"

"Nothing to tell. No copy. No record player. Ancient history." And with that, Vernon retreated back in his shell.

"But surely copies exist," I said.

"What makes you so sure?"

"Just guessing."

"Look, buddy, I'm tired of your guessing and I'm tired of your questions. I know Miss Essie meant well by bringing you in here. I appreciate how Miss Essie worries after me. But mostly I appreciate my privacy. So if you wouldn't mind . . ."

"Don't mind at all," I said. "I'll be on my way. But if you ever feel the need for company, just holler. I could come over with my guitar and we could—"

"Thanks but no thanks."

"Or if you wanna hear a little of my music, I'll be down at Big Bill's on weekends."

Rather than reply, Vernon leaned his guitar against the mattress and, with those long, strong arms of his, moved across the room and saw me to the door.

"Good night," I said.

He nodded and said nothing.

I drove home, thinking that was the end of that. I guessed wrong again.

PRETTY PAPER

Big news: Nutsy Perkins was busted for running the biggest bookmaking operation in Texas. Brother Paul said it happened because Nutsy, a notorious skinflint, failed to give the prosecuting D.A. a piece of the pie. The bar stool where Nutsy sat at Big Bill's remained glaringly empty.

"Don't cry for Nutsy," said Big Bill. "He'll be out in a month. His big-time lawyer, Norby Green, owns half the judges in the city."

Meanwhile, every time that foxy Barbara Lou waltzed in the club, Brother Paul kept her away from me. He didn't buy her claim that she and her old man had split up for keeps. Seeing how she poured herself into a pair of skintight jeans, I myself was ready to believe her. But Brother Paul knew better.

The Big Bill gig went on through February into March. Once in a while, before my first set, I'd stop by Chester's Chili Rice. I'd always ask Essie how Vernon was doing.

"Knock on his door and see for yourself," she'd urge, but I knew that would be pointless.

So you can imagine my surprise when, on one of those occasions that I dropped in for a double chili rice and extra-large lemonade, Chester shouted back to his wife and said, "Essie, look who's here. Didn't you say Vernon had something for this man?"

"Sure did," said Essie, wiping her hands on a towel. "Got it right here under the counter."

"What is it?" I asked.

"It's a big pile of papers. Vernon said to give it to you next time you came in."

"He said that?"

"Guess he thought you'd be interested in whatever's written on these pieces of paper."

"Who wrote it?" I asked.

"Don't know, but I'm guessing Vernon."

Essie reached beneath the counter and pulled up a big pile of papers tied together by a string. The papers were in different colors—blue, red, orange and green.

There had to be over a hundred sheets. The top sheet was white and had only one word written in a large script: VERNON

"I can take this home?" I asked.

"He said it was for you," Essie answered. "I have to believe that he wants you to read it."

Essie put the pages in a shopping bag and handed it to me. I took it to the gig that night and put it in my guitar case for safekeeping. When I got home, I was too tired to start reading. But the next morning, after a couple of cups of coffee, I untied the string that bound the pages and began.

Vernon's penmanship was big and bold. His letters slanted to the right and reminded me of musical notes. I'm no literary critic, but his writing had a rhythm that made it easy to read. His style was direct. I could hear his voice loud and clear. Making it even more interesting was the way he used different-colored paper to match up with his different moods. When he was down in the dumps, he wrote on blue paper. When he was angry, he switched to red paper. When he was happy, he used yellow paper. The different colors mirrored his different mind-sets. It was like looking at a rainbow of feelings. The paper stock itself was thick. It was the kind of heavy construction paper kids use to draw on. It felt good in my hands. I half expected to find drawings along with his words, but there were none. Only word pictures. Vernon chose his words carefully. It reminded me of the way he played the blues. Every note counted. Every word counted. He was serious about telling his story. Once I started reading, I couldn't stop. I kept thinking . . . *all this pretty paper . . .*

I've tried writing this as a song, 'cause songs are the easiest things for me to write. But a song can only say so much. A song lasts just a few minutes. I need more time than that. I need to take my time to say what I need to say. I need to remember that back in school, I got high marks at reading and writing. My teachers said I knew how to express myself. In junior high, Mrs. Hatcher, my English teacher, said I was a natural-born storyteller. Well, the longer this story stays inside me, the more it hurts and the more damage it does. I admit it; I'm feeling damaged. That's why I'm starting on this piece of paper that's the color of ocean blue.

I've been feeling blue—been feeling like I'm drowning—for so long that sometimes I believe I was born that way. But I wasn't. I was born in sunshine. Mama said I was born at high noon on the most beautiful May day of the year. So right now I'm switching to yellow.

This yellow paper is the right paper to describe Grandma, the woman who raised me. Grandma was always smiling. Her real name is Joy—Joy Goodson. Grandma would say, "Sad can't stick around when Happy shows up. And Happy is here to stay." It's amazing that she talked that way because her husband, Harry Goodson, didn't stick around. He left when I was five. Later I learned that he and a neighbor woman ran off to Oklahoma. You'd think such a thing would crush Grandma's spirit, but it didn't. "It isn't *my* spirit that keeps me going," she'd say. "It's *God's* spirit. God keeps us running in the right direction."

My mom and dad ran off four years before Grandpa did. Those were the days of the Great Depression. Texas got hit hard. My folks saw Texas as a lost land and went to California. They decided I'd be better off with Joy, Mom's mom, and they were right. Grandma was my heart. She had a small place right on the outskirts of Round Rock, a Texas town twenty miles north of Austin. Grandma worked as a cook at the local Luby's Cafeteria. Every year at the country bake-offs, her cornbread, pumpkin pie and chili rice won first prize.

Grandma was upbeat. She didn't know fear. "The Good Book says a perfect love casts out all fear," she'd quote. "I'm not saying my love is perfect, but God's love is. All He can do is love. God don't know nothing but love."

Love wasn't all I knew. I also knew envy, which is why I'm writing on green paper. Green is the color of envy. I had lots of envy. I envied kids who had brothers and sisters. I envied kids who lived in big houses, and in high school, I envied kids who had their own cars. I envied kids whose parents owned real farms with horses and cows, not like Grandma's little scrawny plot of land with a few chickens running around. To keep from going hungry, Grandma and I would have to work at adjoining farms, where she'd help out in their kitchens and I'd work in their fields. I envied people who didn't have to do that. I envied families where the mother and father hadn't left their kids behind, families where generations of loved ones lived under the same roof.

I'm using a deeper shade of green paper because the envy got deeper. I couldn't shake it. And even worse, I had to hide the envy because I knew it was wrong. I was ashamed of feeling the way I felt. Grandma scrimped and saved and sacrificed for me. And there I was, bitching and moaning in my secret mind, thinking how I'd gotten a rotten deal cause Mom and Dad had run out to California. I lived for their letters. They came every once in a great while—from Mom, never from Dad. She said they'd opened a car wash in a city called Carson, just outside Los Angeles, but the water pipes burst and they had to close down. That's why they couldn't send me any money.

"Next time," she wrote. But next time never came. Instead of money, she sent a photograph of her and Dad standing in front of some fancy movie palace in Hollywood where the stars had put their footprints in concrete. I couldn't have cared less. "We'll be home for Christmas," she wrote, but come Christmastime there was only another letter with another excuse. And no presents—just a greeting card showing Santa Claus in a Corvette convertible driving down Sunset Strip, wearing wraparound sunglasses and shouting, "Ho Ho Ho from La La Land!"

Envy turned to anger. So I'm turning from green paper to red. I was angry with my parents for living their life without me. And I was angry with my grandmother for not taking her daughter to task. Why couldn't she just call her up and scream, "A good mother doesn't desert her son! You can't do that! Come home and care for him! And tell your husband to do the same!" Why couldn't my grandmother, who was so close to God, invoke his wrath and tell my mother, "God hates you for what you've done! God condemns you! God will send you to hell!" Instead, my grandmother, who couldn't say a bad word about anyone, made excuses for my parents.

"Some people are capable of raising children," she said, "and some aren't."

"Then why did they have me?" I asked.

"It was an act of love."

"Or an accident."

"Every human life is a blessing," she said.

I wanted to say that I felt cursed, but I didn't. I

didn't want to hurt my grandmother. I didn't want to make her think I was ungrateful for all she was doing for me. So I pushed down the anger and went on with my life.

I think of pumpkin orange as the color of Thanksgiving. On this sheet of orange paper, I'm writing down all I can remember about the amazing Thanksgiving when, out of the blue, my mom and dad showed up in Round Rock.

It was the late 1940s. I was a teenager working weekends at the gas station out on the highway when an old Packard pulled in. At first I didn't recognize the man rolling down the window and offering a smile. He had whisky breath and an untamed beard.

"Vernon!" he exclaimed. "Don't tell me you don't know your own father!"

I didn't. I hadn't seen him in five years. I looked over and saw my mother, who was wearing a bright orange dress. She jumped out of the car and ran over to hug me. She'd gotten heavy while Dad was rail thin.

"You handsome devil, you," she said. "My son. My beautiful son."

She was crying and, though I tried not to, so was I.

I filled up their car with gas and paid for it myself. We met up that night at Grandma's. The next day was Thanksgiving.

"I didn't want to tell you they were coming," said Grandma, "on account of sometimes they change their plans. But they're here and tomorrow we'll all be together."

"How long are they staying?" I asked.

"I expect through the holidays."

That Thanksgiving was the first holiday I remember spending with my parents. Watching Mom and Grandma working together in the kitchen made my heart sing. Dad tried talking to me, but booze got in the way. He couldn't keep his thoughts straight. By early afternoon he was so plastered he fell asleep on the couch. He woke up in time to eat the most delicious Thanksgiving meal ever: turkey, stuffing, gravy, cranberry sauce, creamy mashed potatoes, glazed carrots, green beans, hot-water cornbread, buttermilk biscuits and two freshly baked pies—pumpkin and apple—for dessert.

After dinner, Mom announced that she and Dad had decided to leave California and were thinking of relocating to Dallas, only a few hours north of Round Rock, where they were looking to buy a motel that had just gone on the market.

"It even has a swimming pool where you can come and swim whenever you like," said Mom.

The truth is that, even though I was excited to be sharing Thanksgiving dinner with my folks, I really didn't know them. They were strangers. But I still loved the idea of their living nearby. I imagined that I would move into their motel. I'd get a car of my own. Life would be great.

At the end of the evening, Mom gave me a big hug.

"Everything is changing," she said. "Everything is getting better. Now that we're all together, we're gonna stay together."

Dad, who had overeaten, was back on the couch, snoring his head off. When he woke up, he got into a screaming argument with Mom, accusing her of hiding his wallet. His face turned beet red, and I thought he was gonna haul off and hit her. I wouldn't allow that. I'd knock him out before he touched her. Fortunately, Grandma found the wallet and the old man quieted down.

In bed that night I couldn't sleep because of the fantasies dancing through my head. I kept thinking of that motel. Dallas was a big city that always seemed out of my reach. Now, with my parents living there, Dallas would be part of my life. Finally my parents would be part of my life.

But when I woke up the next morning, my parents had already packed their things into the Packard and were fixing to say good-bye.

"Where are you going?" I asked.

"Driving up to Dallas today," said Mom.

"Can I come?"

Mom turned away from me. She couldn't even look at me when she said, "We're staying with some friends while we work out the details on the motel. We need to get settled first. But you'll hear from us. Oh, and before I forget, we left your Christmas gift with Grandma."

"Aren't you gonna be here for Christmas?" I asked.

"Gonna try."

"We need to get going, babe," said Dad.

And then they were gone.

I can't write what happened next on an orange page. I need to go to black and find white ink where my writing can show up.

There won't be much written on this black page. I'll make it simple.

Me and Grandma weren't worried when we hadn't heard from my parents a week after Thanksgiving. That was normal. But then the phone rang and

Grandma answered. As she listened, her eyes seemed to widen. Her eyes, usually calm, had an expression I'd never seen before. I heard the sound of a silent alarm. There was alarm in her eyes. There was panic.

She put down the phone and called me to her side. She put her arms around me and said, "There was a fire. A terrible fire."

"What kind of fire?" I asked.

"A heater exploded in the old house where they were staying. They were sleeping up in the attic and the firemen couldn't get to them in time."

"You mean . . ."

"They're gone, Vernon. They're gone."

On this gray paper I write what I remember of those days. On the day of my parents' funeral, the sky was gray. Grandma's face was ashen gray. The walls of the church were gray. The old preacher had unruly gray hair and spoke in words that made no sense to me. He praised my parents as God-fearing people, a man and woman who loved and cared for their family and friends. But hardly any of their friends had bothered to show up. And the truth was that this minister didn't know my mother or father, who never had even attended his church. He was saying all these things for Grandma. He respected Grandma 'cause Grandma knew God. But my parents didn't.

At that moment, neither did I. God was as gray and lifeless as the corpses in the coffins in front of the pulpit. If God is all good, how did my life turn out all bad? What did I do to deserve these parents? Why did they leave me? And why did they die in a fire? I guessed it was because my father was dead drunk and couldn't help either Mom or himself get out. But I didn't really know, and I didn't really care. So if I didn't care, why was I crying my eyes out? Why was I sobbing uncontrollably? Why did my grandmother have to take me, a fifteen-year-old boy, and cradle me in her arms like a baby? These two people were never there for me to begin with . . . so what difference did it make that they were dead? They'd always been dead to me. I'd been an idiot for believing otherwise. Now no more fooling. Now stark reality.

I know it's a strong word, but I had hatred in my heart. Hatred for my father. Hatred for hypocritical preachers who say beautiful things about dead people who are anything but beautiful. Hatred for life that gives you hope and then turns hope into a cruel joke. Hatred for everything and everyone but my grandmother, who held me close to her, held me in the church, held me in the car driving to the cemetery, held me as we stood in front of the empty graves and watched the coffins sink into the ground. Grandma never let me go.

"I'll never let you go," she whispered in my ear. "I'll never stop loving you, and neither will God."

Grandma, bless her heart, did all she could. After the funeral, she bought a Christmas tree and decorated the house with bright red Christmas flowers. She cooked all my favorite foods. But it was still the saddest Christmas of my life.

It's one thing to be sad during normal days. But during Christmas, the season of good cheer, sadness weighed on me twice as heavy. Didn't help when the carolers came by to sing their songs about baby Jesus. Didn't help to sit in church, listening to some cheerful sermon and seeing happy faces all around me. Everyone's happiness only added to my unhappiness.

It was a long dark winter, the longest and darkest I'd ever known. I kept picturing the fire. I imagined my mother trying to rouse my father from his drunken sleep, trying to drag him from the room, trying to save him, only to . . .

I had to turn off my mind. I had to turn off my imagination. I'd look out the window instead and stare up at the slate-gray sky. Winter dragged on. I thought winter would never end, that for the first time in the history of the world, the seasons would never change.

It would be winter forever, and my frozen heart would never feel warmth again.

I'm writing on pink paper because I'm remembering the sunrise on a spring morning when everything changed. It happened in April. I got up earlier than usual. Something felt different. I looked out the window and saw a streak of pink brighten up the bottom of the sky. I can't tell you why, but watching the darkness lift into light, I could feel my heart lift.

My heart had been lead heavy. The heaviness got increasingly worse because I wasn't talking. I kept it all inside. My grandmother knew to let me be. She knew I was suffering in silence and that no coaxing could get me to open up. So instead of lecturing me or forcing the Bible down my throat, she'd reassure me of only two things—that she loved me, and that God loved me. I knew she did, but I still didn't know about God. I also wondered why Grandma never doubted God, since God hadn't given her such a great life.

The dark cloud of doubt had been hanging over my head ever since my parents' death. In spite of Grandma's efforts, Christmas had been miserable. I hadn't even bothered to open the gift my mother had left for me.

“It’s a big box,” said Grandma. “It must be something wonderful.”

“It’ll just remind me of them,” I said. “I don’t want to be reminded.”

“I understand, Vernon. I’ll put it in my closet. You take your time and open it whenever you like.”

I said very little to Grandma, and at school I said nothing. Everyone knew about the tragedy. I could sense everyone’s pity, and it felt terrible. Pity was the last thing I wanted. Pity seemed to mark me as a pathetic person. I tried to push ahead and forget what had happened. I lost myself in books. Reading *Huckleberry Finn* and *The Call of the Wild* was a way of getting out of Round Rock and living in another world. Make-believe worlds were better than my real world.

“Things change,” Grandma would say over dinner. “Nothing stays the same. Moods change. Seasons change. Good follows bad, like day follows night. Good things will happen to you. But they won’t happen on your time. They’ll happen on God’s time.”

But what good could Grandma possibly be talking about? It was good to be reading history books, but my history teacher’s main interest was coaching basketball. When it came to learning about the American Revolution and the Civil War, he thought I asked too many questions. Mrs. Hatcher, my English teacher, encouraged me to read and write more. But early in March she became sick and had to leave. She was diagnosed with cancer. The woman who took her place was old and cranky, and had no love of literature like Mrs. Hatcher.

I kept up with my job at the filling station. But that was monotonous. Pumping gas, checking oil, washing windshields.

"As long as you stay steady," Grandma would say, "you'll be ready to receive God's gift."

What gift, Grandma? I wanted to ask. *Why should I believe in the fairy tale of a gift-giving God when Mrs. Hatcher is dying of cancer? What's the point of fooling myself?* But I didn't open my mouth. Why hurt Grandma? By keeping all this inside, though, I'm not sure I knew how much I was hurting myself throughout that brutally painful winter.

So on that spring morning when I saw a streak of pink across the sky, I felt something I hadn't felt in months—warmth. Or maybe it was hope. Or maybe it was just happiness that the long chill was ending. I can't explain it other than to say that the dark cloud hanging over my head seemed to be breaking up so that light—this shimmering ribbon of pink light—could shine through.

White paper seems to be the right color to describe that day in detail. White because that was the day when everything suddenly appeared fresh, bright and new. The great event happened early in the morning on the steps of the school building. The girl was walking ahead of me, stumbled and fell back into my arms. I caught her. I held her. Surprised and embarrassed, she looked up at me. Her eyes were emerald green. I had never seen eyes that green before. Her glowing eyes took my breath away. Her eyes seemed to be smiling. She had a sweet little button nose and deep dimples in her cheeks. Her thick blond hair fell over her shoulders and was cut in bangs just a few inches above her eyebrows. Her bangs gave her a mysterious look.

"Sorry" was the first thing she said to me.

"Nothing to be sorry about."

"My first day of school, and I was about to fall on my fanny."

I had to laugh. Girls at our school didn't talk that way.

"Are you new here?" I asked.

"Yes. We just moved from Oklahoma. My name's Marla. Marla Covington. Thanks for saving me."

“I’m Vernon. I didn’t do anything.”

“You were in the right place at the right time. Maybe you can show me around school.”

“Sure thing.”

A pretty girl showing any interest in me was—well, a brand-new world. In my old world I was shy. And a loner. Because I always had to work after school, I could never go out for sports. I was big and strong enough to play football and basketball, but never got the chance. The girls latched on to the athletes. When it came to school parties and dances, I found excuses not to go. Aside from Willard Parsons, who worked at the gas station with me, I really didn’t have any friends at all. Approaching sixteen, not only hadn’t I kissed a girl, I really never had an official date.

And then suddenly on this spring morning Marla, in her white pleated skirt and tight white blouse, came waltzing into my life. She took the lead. She was so easy to talk to I felt that I’d known her in some previous life. As I walked down the hallway with her, pointing out the auditorium and cafeteria and gym, it was like hanging out with an old friend.

“Why are the kids at this school so stuck-up?” she asked.

“Some are, some aren’t.”

“You don’t seem stuck-up.”

"Got nothing to be stuck-up about."

That made her laugh. I couldn't remember making a girl laugh before. Marla laughed easily. Nothing was forced. Everything flowed naturally.

"You better show me to my homeroom."

I was disappointed to learn she and I had different homerooms.

"Hope we have some classes together, Vernon," she said when I left her.

We didn't, but that made me think about her all the more. Other than learning her name and that she was a new student, I didn't know anything about her. I had wanted to say, "Look for me at lunchtime," but I didn't. I had wanted to ask for her phone number, but I chickened out. For the rest of the day, wherever I was, I stretched my neck looking for her. After school, I waited by the main door hoping to see her on her way out, but she never appeared. I felt like I'd lost out completely. But even if I had seen her, I'd've probably just frozen up. She was too good to be true.

I'm changing colors now, going from white to turquoise because turquoise is the blue-green color of surprise and discovery. I need turquoise to remind me of the shock—the beautiful shock—that happened that very evening. It was a Thursday, the night when Grandma worked late at her job.

When I got off from the gas station at seven, I'd walk over to Luby's Cafeteria and eat the leftovers Grandma had saved me. It was only a half mile away. I went in the back door and saw Grandma taking cornbread out of the oven.

"Hi, honey," she said. "You look different."

"I do?"

"You look like you're waiting for something to happen."

Before I could figure out how to reply, Marla walked by carrying a container of green beans.

"Meet our newest helper," said Grandma. "She just came on today. Marla, this is my grandson, Vernon."

My heart beating wildly, I couldn't pretend not to be overjoyed. I was all smiles—and so was she.

"Hey, Vernon, another nice coincidence," said Marla.

"And so you already know each other," said Grandma.

"Only seconds before we met, he had me in his arms," Marla said.

Grandma looked puzzled.

Marla explained, "I tripped walking up the steps to school and he caught me."

"Well, that's Vernon," said Grandma. "Always there when you need him. Best friend you'll ever have."

"I bet that's right," said Marla, looking at me with smiling eyes.

"I'm fixing you a plate right now," Grandma told me. "You hungry?"

"Starved."

I took my food and sat at an empty table at the back of the restaurant, knowing closing time was eight p.m. My plan was to wait till then and see if I could walk Marla home.

"You waiting to see me home?" she asked as she walked by me a few minutes after eight.

"If you want me to," I said.

"It's far. Maybe two miles. You don't have a car, do you?"

"Nope."

"I could call my dad."

"Or we could walk. Weather's nice."

"Okay, let's brave it."

I told Grandma what we were doing and she began to say that she could drive us, but she caught on. She withheld that suggestion and said, "Beautiful night for walking."

"Good night, Mrs. Goodson," Marla said to

Grandma. "Thanks for helping me through my first day on the job."

"You're doing just fine, darling."

"You know something," said Marla, directing her words at both me and Grandma, "I really *am* doing just fine."

As we started walking, Marla drew close to me. Our arms were nearly touching. Only a fraction of an inch separated us. The half-moon was a yellowish glow. The air was still.

"It's the warmest night of the year," I said.

"It was freezing cold when we left Oklahoma," said Marla.

"Is that where you were born?"

"I was born in Colorado, but we've been moving ever since. Dad's a truck driver. They change his route all the time."

"Changing schools all the time must be hard," I said.

"What's hard is that the day after we moved here, Dad got laid off. So Mom and I have to work. We're broke. We're always broke. I hate being broke."

"We don't have much money either."

"Your grandma's a nice lady. Does she live with you and your folks?"

"It's just me and her. My folks are gone."

"What do you mean, 'gone'?"

I hesitated and then, seeing how Marla liked straight talk, I said, "Dead."

"Oh, wow. I'm so sorry. When did it happen?"

"This past winter. A fire. They were in an old house, trapped in the attic when a heater exploded."

"That's horrible."

"If you want to know the truth—" I began to say before cutting myself off.

"I do want to know the truth."

"I think my father was too drunk to save himself or Mom."

That stopped Marla in her tracks. "Sounds like my dad. He drinks like a fish. He even drinks on his long hauls. I'm always scared he's gonna run off the road and take some poor innocent soul with him."

In these few seconds, I had shared information with Marla that I hadn't shared with anyone. And in turn, she was completely candid with me. I wanted to tell her how much her honesty meant to me, but I didn't. For a few seconds we just stood there in silence. I waited until she started walking again. I stayed close by her side. We passed by the Dairy Queen, which, was closing up for the night. Down the street, the 7-Eleven was still open.

"Want a candy bar?" Marla asked.

"Sure."

"I'm buying," she said. "Snickers okay?"

"I like Snickers."

"One Snickers for two," she told the man behind the counter.

She tore off the wrapper and offered me a bite.

"Thanks," I said.

"You have sisters and brothers?" she asked as we walked on.

"No. How about you?"

"Only child. Spoiled child."

"You don't seem spoiled," I said.

"You don't know me."

"I want to."

I want to—those three words unexpectedly fell out of my mouth. They seemed so pushy. They didn't seem like anything I'd say to a girl. But I said them because I meant them. I might have also said: *I know this is crazy, I know we just met, but I love you, I love everything about you, I love the way you look, the way you talk, the way you're so honest and relaxed and unworried, I love the way it feels to be walking next to you, I love being in your company, I love how you just fell into my life, fell in my arms, I love how we wound up alone on this dark road behind the farmers' market and the way the light of the moon is making me feel like we're walking through a dream, a beautiful dream where for the first time ever, I feel close to a beautiful girl who doesn't intimidate me or make me uncomfortable, who gives me the courage to reach out and just touch her cheek.*

I did that. I actually reached over and touched her cheek. She smiled and reached over and touched mine.

We stopped and she said, "It's been a great day so far. It's been a great night. And I honestly think we both feel like kissing. So we might as well just go on and do it. Why not?"

I didn't hesitate. When our lips met, I closed my eyes. She opened her mouth so our tongues could touch. I tasted chocolate. My heart was hammering. It was the sweetest moment of my life.

I know red represented anger before, but now I'm writing on red paper for different reasons. Red also reminds me of desire. Like most teenage boys, I had strong desires before, but Marla took it to a whole different level. Marla threw me into a tailspin.

That night, I couldn't sleep. When I walked her to the door of the small run-down house on the outskirts of town that she shared with her folks, she moved us into the shadows so we could kiss again. Our second kiss lasted longer than the first. During our second kiss, she pressed against me so I could feel the fullness of her breasts. She felt how much I wanted her, and she didn't back away. She liked how I'd grown excited. She was excited. She said, "You made this the best day ever. I hated the idea of moving here and not knowing anyone and having to look for an after-school job. But right away I found a job and made a friend. Now I see that everything's gonna be great." And with a final kiss, she sent me on my way.

The heat of that kiss had me tossing and turning. I can't say why, but something inside told me to finally go in the closet and open the Christmas present that had been sitting there since my mother had given it to me before Christmas. I tore off the paper and saw it was a Stella Harmony acoustic guitar. The neck was a dark brown. The curved body was sunburst wood. What happened next has to be written in yellow.

I cradled the guitar in my arms, strumming the strings until the sun came up and, shining through the curtains, lit my room in golden happiness. In my mind, holding the guitar was like holding Marla. I didn't know how to play it and didn't know any songs, but that didn't stop me from trying to figure it out. I tried to form a melody. I made up some silly words. Even though the process was new, I felt comfortable working my way around the instrument. It didn't feel at all awkward or strange.

I knew that my friend Willard also owned a guitar. His uncle, a musician in Austin, had promised to teach him to play. Willard once said something about putting together a band. Willard was always making plans. He was a six-foot-two laid-back blond-hair blue-eyed kind of guy who was good at about everything he tried. At the gas station where we worked together, he was the best mechanic. At school he made the best grades. He was also the fastest sprinter on the track team. And at the time I met Marla, the first girl to show any interest in me, Willard had already dated three of the prettiest girls at school. His current steady, Cynthia Simone, was head cheerleader.

I'm seeing a green light, so I'm writing on green paper. Green says, "Get going, put the pedal to the metal, full speed ahead."

Two weeks flew by. I saw Marla every day at school. Every night I walked her home from work. We kept kissing in the shadows. Didn't take long to go beyond the kissing. While I was unschooled, she was experienced. In matters of sweet love, she showed me the way.

Love and music were all mixed together in my mind. The closer I grew to Marla, the more attached I became to my guitar. By listening to songs on the radio, I could follow along and pick out the melodies. It came easier to me than I would have ever imagined. I was amazed by my progress.

Willard was the first one I told.

"Guess what," I said. "I got a guitar."

"Great. Time to put a band together."

"But I'm just a beginner."

"Me too. But Uncle Skeeter can teach us. He's coming up this weekend. You still seeing that girl Marla?"

"Yeah."

"She's a knockout, but wonder if she can she sing?"

"I haven't asked her."

"Ask her. Cynthia's been taking violin lessons for years. She can really play the fiddle. She'd join the band in a minute. A two-guy, two-girl band with two pretty girls—man, we can't miss."

When I walked Marla home from work that night, I brought up the subject.

"I know this is a funny question," I said, "but can you sing?"

"That's not a funny question. That's a good question. And the answer is yes. I love to sing. You should hear me sing in the shower."

The idea thrilled me. This whole mix of sex and love and making music thrilled me. And when I met Willard's Uncle Skeeter, the thrills all came to life.

Skeeter Jarvis needs a blue sheet of paper because the first thing he talked about was the blues.

"I can play honky-tonk," he said while tuning his guitar. "I can play bluegrass. I can play jazz. I can play any damn thing you like. But I'm a bluesman, boys, 'cause the blues are the bottom line. Scrape off the fancy dressing, cut out the fat and what do you got? You got the crux of true-life music, and that's the blues."

It was a warm day in May and we were sitting in Willard's backyard—just Willard, me and Skeeter, a man who looked to be in his mid-sixties. His long face was weatherworn. Full head of gray hair, big ears, big bulging eyes, lanky build, long arms, long fingers, long fingernails. Big sly grin. And an unlit hand-rolled cigarette stuck in the corner of his mouth. I figured it was tobacco. I figured wrong.

"I ain't gonna smoke this shit in the presence of

you young men," he said. "Especially not in the presence of my nephew. I'm not gonna recommend it, but I'm not gonna lie and act like I don't like it and don't see it as something a whole lot better than that gut-wrenching whisky that turns sane men crazy. I've seen whisky turn peaceful souls into cold-blooded killers. I've seen whisky destroy the lives of God-fearing women. Why, a mere half-pint can turn a saint into a sinner. This here weed has none of those devilish properties. All it does is let me relax and that, boys, is what the blues are all about. Like ol' Lightnin' Hopkins himself once told me, 'You play the blues to lose the blues.' So I'm just gonna start off by playing me some blues."

Skeeter leaned back on this rickety wooden folding chair and played a salty string of notes that shot right down from my head to my heart. My heart got warm all over. I'd heard blues on the radio by John Lee Hooker, whose popular songs like "Boogie Chillen" I'd recently begun to learn by ear. But Skeeter, who played on a beat-up archtop blond Gibson acoustic that he said was over fifty years old, offered up a purer deep-down Delta version of the blues—simple but filled with feeling. After noodling around awhile, he reached down and put on a neck rack that let him blow his silver harmonica while at the same time he picked his guitar. This went on for a while—leaning into his mouth harp, plucking those strings. He was giving us a private show, and we were eating it up.

When he finally came up for air, I asked him about the bottleneck that he had slipped on his finger. He answered with a deluge of stories about Bukka "Bottleneck" Dupree, the black man who'd taught him everything he knew.

"That's why I'm schooling you boys," he said. "I'm schooling you the way Bottleneck schooled me. I'm starting with the blues."

When it came time for our instruction, both Willard and I, guitars in hand, sat in folding chairs across from Skeeter.

"Just follow me," said Skeeter. "I'll start the line, and you finish it."

Skeeter played a blues line and I followed, but Willard stumbled.

"You thinking too much, son," Skeeter told his nephew. "Don't think. Just shut your eyes and let the feeling come out."

"But I need to know where to put my fingers," Willard protested. "I need to see what notes to play."

Willard struggled—this was the first time I'd seen him struggle with anything—while I soared. It wasn't that I was trying to excel. I was just doing what came naturally. Skeeter heard what was happening and dealt with his nephew patiently. He showed him lots of love. He got him to strum simple rhythm guitar while giving me room to solo. I'm not saying my solos were all that great, but they did seem to make sense.

"Just tell the story, son," Skeeter egged me on. "Just say what you got to say."

A few minutes later, in spite of what he'd said earlier, he lit his joint, inhaled and started talking about singing. "Now, any man who plays guitar gotta put his voice to it," he declared, his words starting to slur a bit. "You gotta sing because talkin' is okay, but singin' is better. Singin' is talkin' made pretty. Birds sing and we love 'em for it. Talkin' gets tired, but singin' stays new. Singin' calms down that devil inside us. Mama don't talk us to sleep. She sings us to sleep. She don't talk no lullaby, she sings it. You don't talk no love out of a lady. You sing it out of her. You sing her into your song. You boys follow?"

We nodded.

"I can sing," Willard said. "I like to sing."

"I know you can, and if you're gonna have a band, you might just do the singing, especially if your buddy here keeps burning up that guitar. You ever hear of Tommy Duncan?"

Of course we had.

"Tommy's the piano player and singer for Bob Wills and the Texas Playboys. Smoothest singer ever. Except for Jimmie Rodgers. That man could yodel. I could sing you some of his songs so you can feel what I'm talkin' 'bout."

"Maybe we should think about someone more up-to-date than Jimmie Rodgers," Willard suggested.

Skeeter didn't like the suggestion. "Now, that's the problem with you young folks. Don't care nothing about what came before. Only interested in what's ahead. Well, I say you can't get ahead without looking back. See what worked then. Then figure out how to rejuggle it so as to make it your own. That's the smart way. That's why we got history books to study. Except in this here case we don't need a book since you got history standing right here in front of you. You got me. I done played with Bob Wills. I done harmonized with Tommy Duncan. I rode the rails with Jimmie Rodgers, the Singing Brakeman. I sang the blues with Leadbelly. I watched these men make people happy with their music. That's the key, boys—making people happy. You do that and you'll never have to work a day in the fields or waste your life in some factory."

I believed Skeeter's every word. I believed him not only because his words made sense but because of the music that accompanied his words. He played while he spoke. His fingers ran over the guitar with such ease that I could only marvel. He inspired me to go off and practice. From then on, I practiced all the time. I practiced at school during lunch. I practiced at work at the gas station when business was slow. I practiced when Marla and I took long walks into the woods outside town. We had our hidden spots—an abandoned barn, a secluded meadow—where I practiced before we made love. Then I practiced after we made love. Marla would sing along while I practiced. I was getting good enough to pick out popular songs we heard on the radio, like Dinah Shore's "Buttons and Bows." Marla could match her voice perfectly to the melody. Her singing voice had the same cuteness—the same coyness—as her speaking voice. When Skeeter heard her, he said, "She's a natural. Both of y'all are naturals."

I'm still using green paper because I'm feeling the let's-get-going excitement of those first days of falling in love with Marla and music. It all happened together. It all happened magically. Marla brought out the music and the love in me, and she swore I did the same for her. Grandma also loved Marla and was convinced that God had brought her to me. Marla's parents were less enthusiastic about our courtship. Her mom was a pretty woman who seemed sad all the time and stayed in her bedroom with the curtains drawn. Her dad was mostly gone. The few times I met him, he had nothing to say to me and never looked me in the eye. He reminded me of my own father.

Skeeter Jarvis really became our father. He was our teacher and our ringleader, an old man with a young heart. When Willard got his dad to give him the old family Hudson, the four of us started driving down to Skeeter's place in East Austin.

He was a lone white man living on the black side of town. His ramshackle house was filled with old instruments. He said he repaired the instruments of the most famous musicians in Texas, but I never saw any of those musicians at his house. I also wondered why, given how good he was, he wasn't in a band. He said he was. He said he was alternating between three or four bands, but he never invited us to hear him. Only later did I learn from Willard's dad—Skeeter's brother—that Skeeter, for all his bragging, had a crippling phobia about playing in front of more than three or four people. He was stricken with stage fright. Maybe that explains why he devoted all this crazy energy to prepare us to perform in public. He needed to get us to do what he couldn't.

Every band has its own strange chemistry, and ours was no different. Among four people, talent and drive are not evenly distributed. Everyone knew that I'd become Skeeter's protégé, just based on how quickly I'd learned his lessons. Because it seemed only fair, I was happy to let Willard, who'd switched over from guitar to bass fiddle, do the singing along with Marla. Their voices matched up in a pleasing manner. Willard's pitch wasn't as good as Marla's, but good enough. They got along great. To see them singing together, you'd think they were an actual couple in love.

Cynthia could play decent fiddle. Besides, in those days a girl fiddler was a novelty—especially a raven-haired beauty like Cynthia. I liked Cynthia. She was popular for a reason. She was a nice girl with a good heart. There were times, though, when Cynthia got jealous of the tight harmony between Marla and Willard, but Willard reassured her that they were play-acting. It was a musical act and nothing more than make-believe romance.

Skeeter also found us a drummer, a short red-haired kid our age nicknamed Sticks. Sticks had lots of nervous energy. He played in a high school marching band. He also worked as Skeeter's instrument repair apprentice. And best of all, he had his own set of drums. Sticks didn't say much, but he had a positive energy and a strong beat.

Willard, Marla, Cynthia and I had one powerful thing in common. We liked attention. Marla and Cynthia were more than just pretty girls. They were knockouts who knew the effect they had on the opposite sex. In their snug sweaters and skirts, in their Western boots and frilly earrings, they loved being onstage. Same for me and Willard. Because he's a handsome guy, standing tall as he plucked the bass, Willard attracted the girls. I attracted the people who were into music. Progressing by leaps and bounds, I was eager to show off my new skills.

We called ourselves Good Friends. Wasn't a fancy or clever name, but it fit. We *were* good friends. Marla and Cynthia had become close, in spite of the fact that Cynthia still worried that Willard had feelings for Marla. I could have worried about that same stuff, but I put it out of my head. I stayed focused on the music.

We followed Skeeter's advice when he said our first gigs should be homegrown. "Play for your schoolmates and friends," he urged. "Get the people you live with to like you. Make sure the home crowd is behind you."

That's just what happened. When we played local

high school dances, we were a hit. Skeeter had made sure we could cover a lot of the current hits—like Hank Snow's "I'm Movin' On" and Lefty Frizzell's "If You've Got the Money, I've Got the Time." Marla sang a version of the Andrews Sisters' "I Can Dream, Can't I?" and she and Willard dueted on Teresa Brewer's "Music! Music! Music!" But Skeeter also encouraged me to write. He saw that I had the ability.

"It's good to be able to copy songs from the radio," he said. "Everyone loves hearing those songs. But if you ever wanna have your own song on the radio, you're gonna have to write it."

"How do I do that?" I asked. "Never have really written before."

"Have you ever dreamed?"

"Sure."

"Well, all that stuff that happens in your dreams, all those stories you're making up in your mind—that's writing."

"It is?"

"Hell, yes. That's pure creativity, boy. Proof that the mind is a fountain of ideas that won't ever dry up. Only thing stopping the mind is overthinking. When you try too hard. When you rack your brain. When you stop thinking and stop racking and get to relaxing, why, the ideas just pour out of you."

"They do?"

"They will, Vernon. You'll see."

I saw. And what I saw turned out to be one of the biggest surprises of my life. Ideas came to me just the way Skeeter predicted. That's why I'm writing on yellow paper. When I see yellow, I see lightbulbs bright with ideas.

The best ideas came to me when I was with Marla. She was at our house more often than her own. Grandma had become her second mother. Grandma wouldn't even object if she went with me into my bedroom—as long as we left the door open. I'd be on my bed, guitar in hand, and Marla would be sitting across from me, our toes touching. I'd start strumming and Marla would start humming.

"This guitar stuff is too easy for you," she teased. "You need to get a harder instrument, like a tuba. I'd like to see you lugging a tuba around town."

"I'd make you carry it for me."

"Good luck with that."

"I'm sticking with guitar," I said.

"All right, then play something pretty."

I plucked a pretty melody out of pure air.

"What do you think?" I asked.

"I like it—if the song's gonna be about me."

"All my songs are about you."

"I know, but this one, this pretty one, this one has to be *especially* about me."

"Used to be sad," I began to sing, wedding the words to the notes, *"used to be lonesome and blue . . . then someone came along . . . someone like you . . ."*

"Someone *like* me, or me?" asked Marla. "I don't want you wanting someone *like* me. I want you wanting *me*."

"Of course the someone is you," I said. "Who else could it be? Lemme start over again."

I took the same notes and sang over them. *"Used to be sad . . . used to be lonesome and blue . . . didn't know what love was . . . till I found you."*

"That's better," said Marla.

"Let me go on. Let me sing . . . *thought I'd be alone the rest of my days . . . living life in a dark foggy haze . . ."*

"That sounds too sad," Marla interrupted.

"People like sad songs. But this sad song turns happy. Listen to this . . . *the fog done lifted . . . the sun's shining through . . . and it's all because . . . God gave me you."*

"You sure you want to bring God into it?"

“That line will make Grandma happy. Besides, what do you have against God?”

“You were the one who said you really weren’t a believer.”

“That was before I met you. That’s the whole point of the song.”

“Will you call it ‘Marla’s Song’?”

“Why not?”

“But then you gotta mention me in the lyrics.”

“What rhymes with Marla?”

“Let’s ask Willard. He’s the one who’s gonna sing it.”

“Maybe not, Marla. Maybe I’m gonna sing this one.”

“I can hear Willard singing it. He’s the one with the big voice. You saw what happened when he sang ‘Mule Train’ the other night. The girls went wild.”

“This is a softer song,” I said. “It’s a love song that needs to be sung by someone in love.”

“Willard’s in love with Cynthia,” said Marla.

“Willard’s in love with Willard,” I said.

“Come on, Vernon. You’re talking about your best friend.”

“Nothing against Willard. He’s a great guy. But you know well as me that he’s stuck on himself. He can’t walk past a mirror without taking a long look.”

"What's wrong with that? I'm guilty of doing that."

"You're a girl. Girls are supposed to be vain."

"And that's what's wrong with your song, Vernon. It's all about how you feel about me. But there's nothing about me—nothing about the way I look."

"You look beautiful."

"Then say it in the song," said Marla.

I picked the guitar and revisited the same melody, this time sticking on new lyrics. *"She's prettier than Mona Lisa, prettier than Betty Grable . . . Marla's the princess of my story, the heroine of my fable . . ."*

"Now you're making up a fairy tale," said Marla. "You're making up a silly story."

"I never even had a story till I met you."

"Of course you did. Everyone has a story. You just didn't like yours."

"Stories have to feel real. They have to make you feel alive. Before you, I wasn't feeling anything. I was dead inside."

Marla moved closer to me. She put her lips on mine and whispered, "Keep playing, keep singing, keep saying how you adore me."

"I'll write you another song."

"And then another," she said, "and then another after that."

Can't decide what color papers to use to describe all that happens next: red for the passion and love I felt for Marla; green for the envy and jealousy that crept into our lives; pink for the pretty parties we played—the sock hops and proms; gray for the long cloudy days we spent traveling around from gig to gig; yellow and orange for all the hope we carried in our hearts; and blue—I'll need lots of blue paper—for how it all came to a screeching halt.

I'll start with red.

I had never been in love before. I had felt hardly any love from my mother and none from my father. Besides, they weren't around enough to count. When it looked like I'd get to see my folks more—and latch on to the love I'd been missing—they were dead. Grandma's love was the steadiest in my life. She said she got her love from God, and I really couldn't doubt her. Her husband had left her but that hadn't kept her from loving—loving not just me, but her friends, her neighbors and anyone in need. She showed love by convincing Luby's Cafeteria to feed the hungry once every month. And she prepared and served the meals herself.

Godly love, though, is one thing. Godly love is beautiful. But when you're a teenage boy and those hormones start firing, you start looking for another kind of love. I had never known passionate love, never known romantic love before Marla. She was the first girl to say "I'm yours." She was the first girl to show me the secrets of the female body. And it wasn't just her body—as heavenly as her body was. It was her mind. She was quick and witty and smart as a whip. She was unpredictable and daring. She was sassy and self-centered, but that only made me love her more. When I was with her, I was happy. When we were apart, I was miserable. I needed her by my side every minute of every day. She never left my mind. And at night when I went to sleep, she crept into my dreams. When I awoke, I worried that she too was nothing but a dream—that I really hadn't met her, that she really wasn't my girl. But she was. And because she was, I considered myself the luckiest guy alive.

Green.

Jealousy is like a slithering, slow-moving snake. It hides in the grass, it blends in. You don't even know it's there until it strikes. And then it's too late.

Looking back, I can see that Cynthia was probably

a little jealous of Marla because Marla was a good singer. She kept saying that Willard was coming on to Marla and vice versa. She said that anyone could see that. Well, if that was true, I guess I just wasn't looking.

From time to time, though, I could feel Willard's jealousy of me. By getting good at the guitar, I had won his uncle's admiration. Musically, I was the standout member of the band—and that didn't make Willard happy.

But these were masked feelings. On the surface, Good Friends sailed along. By our senior year in high school, we were playing dances not only in the little towns outside Austin, but in Austin itself. Skeeter started talking about taking us to San Antone and Houston, where he knew people who owned music studios. He thought that a few of the songs I'd written were good enough to record.

Grandma always said I'd be the first in our family to go to college. I hated to disappoint her, but the idea of a music career was too good to resist—especially since me and Marla could pursue that career together. Marla's folks didn't seem to care what she did, as long as she could earn money to help them out. Willard's dad, a corn merchant, believed his brother Skeeter, who said the band had a good shot at making it. It was Cynthia's parents who balked.

Cynthia's mom had been president of a fancy sorority at the University of Texas and expected her daughter to follow suit. When Cynthia quit the band and headed off to college, we got another fiddler to replace her, a friend of Stick's called Jason. Marla liked that. She liked being the only the girl in the band.

Then things changed again when, during Cynthia's freshman year, she got her sorority to hire us to play a dance. When we showed up and she heard how good we'd gotten, she figured she'd made a mistake. She wanted back in. She also learned that Willard, with his roving eye, had been meeting ladies on the road. That made her want back in even more. So, despite her parents' protests, Cynthia up and quit college. Since Jason was a better fiddler than Cynthia, that caused a problem. I wanted to keep Jason, and so did Marla. Ever since Cynthia had become a sorority girl, her friendship with Marla had gone bust. But Willard had the most power because he was the only one with a car. In fact, his dad had traded in the old Hudson and bought him a wood-paneled Ford station wagon. That car was our lifeline, so Willard and Cynthia got their way. Jason was out and Cynthia was back in the band.

A red sheet for a red light outside the little music studio in San Antone. The red light meant we were actually cutting a record. We were recording two songs, both written by me. The first was "Something You Got," a tune, like most of my tunes, about Marla. She sang it. *"I was a lonely soul with nothing to do . . . but everything changed the day I met you . . . you grabbed my attention and cold turned to hot . . . all 'cause of that certain something you got."*

The second song, though, wasn't a love song. It was a song I'd written for Grandma. It was called "Faith." I didn't intend to write it, but it just happened, on a gray lonesome morning in mid-December. We were in Odessa the night before, where we'd played a high school dance. My mind was on the upcoming Christmas season. An early West Texas snowstorm had covered the land and turned the highway into a sheet of ice. The road was closed down to Abilene, our next stop, and me and Marla were alone in our motel room. Marla was still asleep. I was sitting up in bed, pen in hand. I remembered another such morning when I was a little kid. Couldn't have been older than five or six. That week, the principal of our little elementary school had died, a man who had showed great kindness to me. It was my first encounter with death. It was the first time I felt terror.

"Are we all gonna have to die?" I asked Grandma on that morning.

"Yes, sweetheart. I'm afraid so."

Being afraid of the dark, I asked her, "And when we die, what will it be like? Will it be dark? Will it be like turning out all the lights?"

"No, child," she said. "It will be like turning *on* all the lights. There will be more light than you can ever imagine. You will be in God's everlasting light. And that's a light that never goes out. That's the light of love."

"But how you do you know that, Grandma? How can you be so sure?"

"Faith," she said. "I have faith."

Those words came back to me on that bleak Odessa morning. It started out as a postcard to Grandma. I was telling her that after Abilene, we had to drive up the Panhandle to Lubbock and Amarillo before heading home—but we should be back in Round Rock by Christmas. Before signing off, I wrote these words, "Thank you for your faith." I looked at what I'd written and heard a song. I picked up my guitar and played very softly, so as not to awaken Marla. I didn't sing out loud, but mouthed the words that flowed from my heart.

"Thank you for your faith . . . I'm not sure I deserved it . . . thank you for your faith . . . not sure I've preserved it . . . but I know it's a gift . . . I can feel it pure and true . . . thank you for your faith—I'll always have faith in you."

The ice melted and the roads became passable. We drove up to Lubbock and Amarillo, where we performed at holiday parties for kids in the Future Farmers of America. We played songs like "The Tennessee Waltz" that had everyone dancing. Everyone was upbeat. But my mood was different. My mind was on this "Faith" song that I'd begun in Odessa. The song wouldn't leave me alone. I wanted it to be perfect, so I kept rewriting until it was. I finished it the night we drove back to Round Rock. Willard was driving, Cynthia was next to him, and me, Marla and Sticks were in the backseat. I played it over and over again until I drove my bandmates crazy.

"Doesn't sound like the kind of song we could play at a dance," said Willard.

"It's a downer," said Marla.

"I don't hear a beat," said Sticks.

"Maybe if you change the words to make it more

like a love song," said Marla out loud before whispering in my ear, "and make it about me."

"It's about Grandma," I said. "It isn't for the band. It's just for her."

"I think it's sweet," said Cynthia. "I think it's beautiful."

Other than Cynthia, no one had anything good to say about the song.

We arrived home December 24, in time for everyone to spend Christmas Eve with family. Willard dropped off Sticks, then Marla, then Cynthia, then me. It was early evening. Grandma was still at work. Luby's Cafeteria closed at eight, so I knew she'd be home by eight thirty. I couldn't wait to play her this song. This was a Christmas gift I knew she'd love. By nine o'clock, though, she still wasn't home. I got worried. I decided to run over to Luby's and see what was wrong. It was cold and overcast. No moon, no stars. The faster I ran, the more fright I felt. My heavy breath looked like trails of smoke in the frosty night air. My fright turned to panic. I tried to calm down. Sometimes there were extra chores Grandma had to do. There had to be a reasonable explanation. No reason to panic. But as I picked up my pace, my panic got worse. I felt panic in my gut, panic in my head. The panic was lifted a little when I saw Grandma's Chevy in her usual parking space. I ran to the front door of the cafeteria. It was locked. I saw Lee, the custodian, mopping the floor and tapped on the window. He came and let me in.

"Where's my grandmother?" I asked.

His troubled eyes said it all. "They had to take her to the hospital, Vernon."

"Why? When? What was wrong?"

"She fell down. She was back there in the kitchen around six o'clock when, just like that, she collapsed on the floor."

Before Lester could say another word, I was out of there and racing over to the hospital, a mile or so away.

"What room is Joy Goodson in?" I asked the nurse on duty.

"Two-ten. Second floor."

I got there just as Doc Swartz was leaving the room. Doc was the man who had delivered me. He'd been our family physician forever.

I didn't need to hear his words because his eyes spoke first. His eyes said, "She's gone."

I'm writing on blue paper and thinking about the song "Blue Christmas." Elvis sang it later in the

1950s, but it was Ernest Tubb's version that was popular during the time I lost my grandmother. She was only sixty-five, the youngest of four girls who had all died before her.

The church was packed with people of every description—all the folks she worked with at Luby's; dozens of loyal Luby's customers she had served with patient kindness; three black families who lived down the road from us and loved her like one of their own; Mexicans—men and women—who in the early years had worked with her in the cotton fields; the adults who were once children she had taught in Bible class; and all the people she had given free meals, either from the cafeteria line or our own kitchen, because they had fallen on hard times.

I sat on the first pew, inches away from her casket covered in red poinsettias and green and white Christmas flowers. It was just a few days after Christmas. The fragrance from the flowers had me dizzy. I was afraid I'd faint. Marla sat next to me. Willard and Cynthia were in the pew behind us. Grandma's friend, Meg Newberry, sang a hymn called "When Time and Eternity Meet." The words didn't register. Instead, inside my head, I heard Ernest Tubb singing about how it will be a blue Christmas without you, how I'll be so blue just thinking about you. I only half heard

Reverend Olan's eulogy. Everything the reverend said was true—Grandma loved the Lord, she loved people, she followed the Golden Rule, she had a generous and humble heart. He spoke calmly. He was completely composed, while I was on the verge of losing it.

In planning the service, Reverend Olan had asked me to say a few final words about Grandma. I told him I couldn't. When he wanted to know why, I was honest. I said that I didn't think I could hold it together.

"You're a musician, Vernon," he said. "Maybe you could speak through your music."

"Just before she died," I said, "I wrote a song for her."

"Would you sing it, son? Would you honor her with your song?"

"I'll try."

Before the service began, I had placed my guitar underneath an easel that held a large photograph of Joy Goodson as a young woman. Her smile and her eyes had not changed over the years. Her smile and her eyes revealed all the love she held for the world. I thought of the love that she held for me. I thought of how she cared for me when no one else would. I thought of the pain she must have felt when her husband had abandoned her, when my parents had left me and when my mother—her daughter and only child—had died during another horrible holiday season.

I heard the preacher call my name. As I rose up from my seat, Marla squeezed my hand. I got my guitar, took a few seconds to tune it and faced the congregation. I stood in front of Grandma's photograph. I felt her holding me up. I felt her love. I sang . . .

Thank you for your faith
I'm not sure I deserved it
Thank you for your faith
Not sure I've preserved it
I know it's a gift
I can feel it pure and true
Thank you for your faith—
I'll always have faith in you

Back to red paper for the red light in the San Antone music studio.

I was singing "Faith" because I wanted to. Because I had to. I was singing "Faith" over the objection of everyone except Cynthia.

"You got better songs," said Willard.

"Prettier songs," said Marla.

“Happier songs,” said Sticks.

“Songs people can dance to,” said Ring Dawson, the man who owned the studio and the little label he called Ring’s Records.

“Besides,” said Willard, “you ain’t our singer anyway. You got no business singing on this record.”

Only Cynthia was on my side. Only Cynthia said, “It’s a lovely song. And it feels like something Vernon has got to sing. Let him sing it.”

I sang it in one take. Everyone knew I’d nailed it.

Although “Something You Got” was the A side, it was the B side that disc jockeys around Texas started playing. Against all odds, “Faith” became a modest regional hit. “Faith” put Good Friends on the map.

Back to green paper means that Good Friends was moving ahead. Back to green means that “Faith” was a big enough record to get us work outside Texas. Back to green means that Marla said yes when I asked her to marry me.

Christmas had become the season of death—the death of my parents, the death of my grandmother, the death of any hope for happiness if I stayed in Round Rock. I couldn’t wait for the holidays to pass so I could take the band and get the hell out of town. By the second week of January, I'd been able to sell Grandma's house for enough money to buy a big station wagon and, for the first time in my life, put a little savings in the bank. By the second week in February, we were in San Antone cutting "Faith." Even if Cynthia hadn't backed me up, I'd have sung that song anyway. I had to do it for Grandma and close off that chapter in my life. The new chapter that opened—the chapter kicked off by the success of "Faith"—took me by surprise and changed the game.

It wasn't until summer that "Faith" began getting airplay around the state. We were shocked. When the A side—"Something You Got"—was released in March, it sank like a stone. I was sure that our dealings with Ring Dawson were history. And then Cynthia's mother called to say she happened to be in Houston when she heard the B side on the radio. We thought she was confusing it with another song that sounded like "Faith." But then other calls came in from friends and relatives around the state saying the same thing: They were hearing "Faith." Finally Ring himself called to report that he was shipping out a thousand copies of the single to meet the demand.

"Damnedest thing I've ever seen," he said. "Some deejay plays the wrong side of the record in Wichita Falls, and suddenly his phone lights up with requests."

Next thing we know, we were booked on local TV shows in Austin, Abilene and Longview. That meant wearing nicer clothes. We put Cynthia and her mom in charge of that. Our outfits—Western-styled suits in black suede—gave us a classier image. Then Ring, who also ran a booking agency, found us work in places as far away as Fayetteville, Arkansas, and Denver, Colorado. Our first hotel lounge gig was in Reno.

"Nevada? That's where people either lose money or get hitched," I told Marla.

"Is that supposed to be a proposal?"

"You know I want to marry you."

"Then propose the right way," she demanded.

"Which way is that?"

"On your knees."

I fell to my knees.

"How's this?" I asked.

"Now say the right words."

"Marry me."

"It's gonna take more sugar than that. I'm gonna have to hear some pretty words."

I spoke the words. I said I adored her. I called her the most wonderful, beautiful, incredible woman in the world.

"Is that enough?" I asked.

"Enough to give me something to think about."

"You're playing with me."

"Only 'cause I love you. Let's do it in Vegas. We'll get Willard and Cynthia to go along with us."

On a Monday morning in June, in a little chapel across from the Sahara, Marla, myself, Willard and Cynthia stood in front of a justice of the peace dressed up in a clown costume. The neon sign outside advertised FIVE-DOLLAR WEDDINGS.

"How much for a double wedding?" asked Willard.

"Another two bucks," said the clown.

"Deal," said Willard, who loved bargains.

Cynthia was hesitant. Her mom had her heart set on a fancy wedding at an Austin country club.

"We'll have the party there," said Willard. "But we can't let Vernon and Marla get ahead of us."

Sticks was our witness.

Afterward, we went to the Sahara and got silly drunk. Louis Prima and Keely Smith were the lounge act. He sang "Just a Gigolo" and "I Ain't Got Nobody." For some reason his singing made me sad. That same night we booked a two-bedroom suite with a split-level living room. Cynthia and Willard never made it to their bedroom. They passed out on the living room couch.

In our room, Marla stood in front of the window that looked out onto the dark desert.

“When I saw we were being married by a clown,” I told her, “I almost ran out.”

She turned to me and said, “I thought it was funny.”

“Marriage isn’t supposed to be a joke.”

“It isn’t?” she asked.

Gray paper for the gray concrete highway that became our home. The highway never ended.

By the middle of the 1950s, we were road-weary, but we were also seasoned pros. We’d been out there for years and were determined to take it to the next level. “Faith” had sold enough to convince Ring Dawson to let us cut a whole album. I wrote eight new songs—Marla sang five and Willard sang three. None of them hit. Skeeter was in the studio when we recorded and urged me to sing at least one number, but I wasn’t feeling it. For me as a singer, “Faith” was a one-shot deal. Willard had the better voice, no doubt, and I liked the way he sang my songs about looking for love in all the wrong places. Marla had been on my case to write a hit song for her, and God knows I tried.

I wrote heartache songs, happy songs and work songs. The year before Tennessee Ernie Ford hit big with “Sixteen Tons,” I wrote a tune called “Coal

Miner's Heartbreak." Willard did a good job singing it, but the song went nowhere. As a group, I guess you'd have to call us a "one-hit wonder." At best, ours was a regional hit that faded after a while. Not that I was complaining. "Faith" was popular enough to get us out there on a circuit of barrooms and dance halls in the Southern and border states, to where we were able to eke out a living.

Sticks, our steady drummer, had no problem hanging in. Willard, who had dreams of being the next Eddy Arnold or Hank Snow, liked the spotlight. So did Marla, who also had designs on big-time stardom. It was Cynthia who suffered most. I do believe that she loved Willard and, at least for the first years, she shared in our fantasy of show business fortune and fame. But unlike the rest of us, Cynthia came from an upper-class family. She had never been deprived of the creature comforts that our band had to forgo. We barely got by. We had no choice but to crash at the cheapest motels and eat at the cheapest dives. The places we were playing were rough and rowdy. It all came to a head—or more specifically Cynthia's head.

At a sawdust-on-the-floor cowboy barroom in Cheyenne, Wyoming, a fight broke out and a misdirected flying beer bottle caught Cynthia on the forehead and knocked her out. The emergency doctor said she was fine, but she wasn't. The next day she went back home to her mother and two weeks later filed papers for divorce.

Naturally that changed our chemistry. To save money, we decided not to replace her. Cynthia looked good on the bandstand, and she was an okay fiddler, but I knew we could do without her. As for Willard, losing his wife was no big deal. Now there was nothing to stop him from loving on those willing women who came his way.

It was Willard's situation that gave me an idea for a song. I heard it as a duet. I imagined someone like Willard finally free to do what he had always wanted. And then I imagined one of those women wanting to do it with him. A lightbulb went on in my mind that let me see the title—"Willing Woman/Willing Man": He sings: *"I've been hankering for someone new to have a good time . . ."*

She sings: *"I've been hankering too for a man to call mine . . ."*

He sings: *"I need a woman to put out this fire . . ."*

She sings: *"I need a man to meet my desire . . ."*

He sings: *"A willing woman, willing and free . . ."*

She sings: *"A willing man, willing to love me . . ."*

It all came together in a hurry. I was so excited

that I called Ring Dawson in San Antone and ran it down over the phone.

"I can hear Willard and Marla singing it," he said. "Aren't you back in Texas next week?"

"We're in Houston on Monday."

"Then I'll put you in the studio on Tuesday. You got something for the B side?"

"I will by Tuesday."

And I did. Something I called "Dreamin' in Blue."

So we're back to blue paper.

"Dreamin' in Blue," unlike "Faith," wasn't a surprise B side hit. This time, the A side was the good side.

I was especially happy to see that Skeeter was able to come by the studio. He was recovering from a heart attack. We'd heard the bad news from Willard's dad when we were playing Lafayette, Louisiana, a few months earlier. But Skeeter had survived and showed up to do what he always did—encourage us to play our best.

"Two damn good songs," he said when he heard them run down. "That 'Dreamin' in Blue' is a pretty ballad, boy, and Marla does it proud. But that 'Willing

Woman' ditty—man, I think you got yourself a hit there, son. And Willard and Marla, them two sing it like they mean it."

When Skeeter spoke those words, a chill ran up my spine. A terrible thought attacked my mind: Had I written something I had been sensing for years? Had I written a blueprint for my own misery? Had I predicted the future?

Looking back, I can now say that I did. Now it all seems so clear. At the time, though, it was a muddled mess. And it all seemed to happen overnight.

"Willing Woman/Willing Man" hit the bottom of the country charts. It sold just enough to convince Ring to have me write enough new songs to fill up a second album. One of those new songs—"Leavin' Ain't the Last Thing on My Mind"—was another way I read between the lines of my marriage to Marla. It was another way that I predicted the future.

As it turned out, Marla was more than willing to leave. And so was Willard. They left together and, if you can believe it, Ring Dawson helped them do it. Turned out, a Nashville producer liked Marla's voice and saw her prospects as a solo artist. He had assembled a bunch of songs for her written by leading Nashville writers that he claimed would take her to the top. A few of those songs were duets, meaning that Willard could come along for the ride.

Making matters worse was the way it all came down. There were no face-to-face talks, no long discussions. Only a note from Marla that said, "I think you know how I've been feeling. If you didn't, you wouldn't have written the songs you wrote. Willard and I are in love. We've been in love longer than you need to know. I don't need to hurt you anymore. I don't want to hurt you at all, but I have to do what's best and what's right for me. Ring will tell you the rest."

That note was left on my bed in a Memphis motel when I woke up late on a Thursday morning. She and Willard were already gone.

I called Ring, who told me about this new business arrangement that completely cut me out.

"How could you do this?" I said. "You're the one who sang my praises. You're the one who couldn't stop talking about my talent."

"Well, this producer in Nashville has bigger talents working for him. He has bigger connections and bigger money."

"And he's got no use for me at all?"

"He doesn't think he needs you."

"And what do you think?"

"I think like a businessman. I'm getting paid, Vernon. The way I figure, I'm entitled. I've put in my time with you guys and this is my payoff. Far as you're concerned, Vernon, you can find a couple of other musicians. Do that and I'll try and get you work. That's all I can do."

Gray paper for the gray day I went to see Skeeter in Austin.

I was sliding down into the deepest funk of my life—deeper than when my folks were killed, deeper than after Grandma died, so deep that I honestly thought of throwing it all in—my music, even my life. How can life be considered worthwhile when, in one fell swoop, you're screwed over by your wife and your best friend? I couldn't imagine a lower blow. I couldn't imagine picking up the pieces and moving on.

My imagination was doing me in—imagining Marla in bed with Willard, loving him as she had loved me; imagining them singing in a Nashville recording studio; imagining them being promoted by some big-shot producer; imagining the success they would have, the money they would make, the happiness they would find. The more I fantasized about their good fortune, the more I imagined my ruin. And the more my ruin seemed like a reality, the more I had to ask myself whether I was to blame. Hadn't I been naïve? Hadn't I missed the most obvious signs along the way? Hadn't I seen that Marla was secretly hot for Willard? Hadn't I known that she was always out for herself? And—worst of all—wasn't I the one who wrote the damn script? Hadn't I given them the parts they had both wanted to play? She'd always been the willing woman; he'd always been the willing man. "Leavin' Ain't the Last Thing on My Mind" had been on her mind for a while. I knew it, but I just wouldn't admit it. Yet I wrote it. I put it down in black and white. She sang it, and then she did it.

If in my heart I felt hatred for Marla and Willard, I felt even more hatred for myself—for denying the truth that had been staring me in the face for so long. I hated myself for being stupid. I hated myself for being a jerk and a tool. I hated myself for being a loser.

The only person in the world who might understand was Skeeter Jarvis. He was Willard's uncle, but he was my mentor. He was the first person to say I had talent. He never stopped encouraging my playing and writing, and even my singing. He was the nearest thing I had to a father. He was a lot closer to me than to his nephew, and I figured that, no matter what, I could count on him.

I figured right.

I'm picking yellow paper—not the sunshine-bright yellow I've used before, but a pale yellow that reminds me of how Skeeter was able to give me the small shot of hope I so badly needed.

Not long after Marla ran off with Willard, I found my way down to Austin. That's when I learned that Skeeter was no longer living at home. After his heart attack, he'd suffered a stroke and was recovering in a nursing facility off South Congress Avenue. The place was pretty dismal—a single-story building with peeling paint and a long hallway that smelled of disinfectant and piss. Skeeter shared a small room with a man who looked like he'd died some time ago.

"He may be dead," said Skeeter. "The nurses don't come 'round often enough to notice."

Seated in a wheelchair, Skeeter could still speak, but couldn't use his left leg.

"They called it a mild stroke. But I call it a stroke of damn good luck."

"Why do you say that?" I asked.

"'Cause it made me grateful for something I took

for granted. Made me count my blessings. You see, son, I can still pick that guitar. Long as I can finger my guitar, I can get through anything, even this godforsaken place."

I understood what Skeeter meant. What looked like mental patients—wild-eyed women in housecoats—were walking the halls talking to themselves. A morbidly obese man came in Skeeter's room, his mouth covered with drool, and sat on the floor.

"I need company," he said.

"I need to get out of here," Skeeter said to me. "There's a patio in the back. Roll me out there, will ya?"

I wheeled Skeeter to a small patch of grass. I took a folding chair and sat next to him. Puffy clouds moved across the afternoon sky. The air was chilly. Skeeter wore a wool ski cap with the word UNDEFEATED written across the front. The lenses of his glasses were dirty.

"Glad you came to see me, Vernon," he said. "I heard what happened."

That made it easier. That meant I didn't have to explain. Before arriving here, I worried whether I could actually tell him the story. In truth, I hadn't told anyone. There wasn't anyone to tell.

"You been hit hard," said Skeeter, whose voice,

despite sounding frail, was still self-assured. "I been hit hard. That's the world. Shit happens. You get a heart attack. You get a stroke. Your wife runs off with your pal. You feel the world's against you. You feel like you been had. And you have. We've all been had. We're all born to die. It's just a matter of how you gonna live and, when the time comes, how you gonna die. Well, son, I know my time's coming soon. I'm looking death in the face, and you know what I'm seeing?"

"No."

"I'm seeing a song. I'm seeing a song about an ol' geezer like me who's scared to death. Who's scared *of* death. And rather than rattlin' on with some stupid philosophy, I just pick up my guitar and turn the whole mess into a tune the whole world can whistle. Go fetch me my guitar, Vernon. It's back in my room."

I got Skeeter's guitar and handed it to him. He held the instrument cautiously. I worried whether he had the strength to play. I worried that he might drop it to the ground. But he held on. His fingers, once lightning fast, moved slowly but deliberately. Each note counted. And his voice, with all its shakiness, touched my heart.

"I call it 'Easygoing,'" he said, "and it 'bout explains everything that needs explaining."

With his eyes closed, he sang:

You get to the end of the road
And wonder why
You're battered, you're bruised
And start to cry:
"What did I do to deserve this fate
That all adds up to a big mistake?"
The answer's not in some fancy prayer
The answer, my friend, is everywhere
The sun comes up, the sun drops down
Seasons change while the world spins round
You're born, you live, and then you die
And all the time you wonder why
You never know why and that's okay
'Cause the mystery ain't going away
Love the mystery and you're sure to find
An easygoing peace of mind
Easygoing when it's good
Easygoing when it's bad
Easygoing when you happy
Easygoing when you sad
Easygoing even when things go wrong
Easygoing like this easygoing song

Skeeter stopped singing and started smiling.

"Make any sense, son?"

I didn't know how to answer. I wanted to say that

his song didn't change the fact that I didn't have Marla and was still messed up. But before I could say that, I realized that when he was singing I wasn't thinking of Marla or of me. I was just hearing this simple bluesy melody and this easy-to-understand message. I guess that was the whole point.

"The whole point, Vernon," he said, reading my mind, "is that you do what you can do. Gardeners dig gardens. Truckers drive trucks. Pickers pick guitars. So pick up your damn guitar and quit whining. Hell, what's happened to you in the last couple of weeks is enough to give you ten years' worth of good songs. Go write 'em, son. Go write 'em while the pain's still fresh."

Guess I gotta go from light yellow to bright yellow paper 'cause I left the nursing home that day knowing I'd been given a good reason not to do myself in. The reason was writing. Basically Skeeter was saying that you can live with anything long as you can write about it. And he wasn't just saying that. He was doing it. If he could keep his spirits up after all the sickness he'd suffered and keep from going crazy in that run-down nursing home, why couldn't I?

I hadn't had a heart attack or a stroke. I wasn't an

old man looking at death. I was a young man looking at life. Had my health. Had a little savings in the bank. Had a car that ran, legs that walked, a mind that thought. My mind had been muddled before I went to Skeeter, but now my mind was clear. My mind could see the truth of what he said.

Writing will keep you from going nuts.

Writing will save you.

So this is my way of saving myself. This is my writing. This is my way of staying sane. This is the story that, by telling it, can't do me any more harm. I'm releasing it. I'm sending it up into the sky. I'm putting it out there so it can no longer put me down.

I'm writing so I can set my troubled soul free.

GONE

"Gone? What do you mean, Vernon's gone?" I asked Chester.

"Damnedest thing," he said. "Soon as me and Essie got back from church this evening—we been there the better part of the day—we found this note. You can read it if you wanna."

Dear Essie and Chester,

Words can't express the gratitude I feel for you both. I call you saints. I loved living here, but it's time to move on. When I get settled, you'll hear from me again. Until then, though, please accept my deepest love.

Your friend for life,
Vernon

"We went back to his room," said Chester, "and all his stuff—his papers and pencils and notebooks—everything was gone."

"How could he move out on his own?" I asked.

"A neighbor said someone came by with a van and helped him. Said it was a woman."

"A young woman?"

"Neighbor said it was a pretty woman. Maybe a relative."

"According to his story, he doesn't have any relatives," I said. With both hands I was holding his stack of pretty paper.

"You read all that?" asked Essie.

"I did."

"What'd it say?"

"It says . . . well, it says a lot of things. But mainly it says he's had a hard time."

"And how did he lose his legs?" asked Chester. "Did he talk about that?"

"He didn't."

"He's the mystery man," said Chester.

"But a good man," added Essie. "A loving man."

"I need to find him," I said.

Why did I need to find him?

Well, for one thing, I had to know what happened next. Where'd Vernon go after he left Skeeter Jarvis in Austin? What became of Marla and Willard? Did Vernon form another band? Did he have any success? How did he wind up in his present condition? And, for God's sake, why did he cut off the story in midstream? What was the point of leaving me hanging?

"So you really have no idea where he could be?" I asked Chester.

"None. He's the Lone Ranger."

"And no friends who would know?" I asked.

"Only you," said Essie.

"Hardly a friend," I said.

"A friend is someone who cares," Essie explained. "I know you care. I think he knows that too."

"Well, if you hear anything, will you let me know?" I asked the couple, scribbling my phone number on a scrap of paper and handing it to them.

"Naturally," said Essie. "But if you catch up with Vernon first, tell him he always has a home here. Tell him that Essie and Chester love him like a son."

"I'm sure he knows that. Maybe I should leave his story with you."

"No," Essie quickly replied. "He wanted you to have it. You keep it. Maybe there's a clue in there about where we might find him."

"Maybe," I said.

I left Chester and Essie feeling all sorts of frustration. Usually I can lose my frustrations by playing music. But it was a Sunday night and that meant no gigs. So I went home. I got there in time to tuck the kids in bed and sing them their favorite lullaby that really wasn't a lullaby at all but a song I'd heard "Guitar Boogie" Smith play called "Redheaded Stranger." While I was singing it, I remembered what Skeeter had told Vernon: *You don't talk kids to sleep. You sing 'em to sleep.*

Having a hard time falling asleep, I picked up Vernon's pretty papers and read 'em all over again, looking for clues about where he might have gone. Couldn't find a one.

Come Monday evening I was back at Big Bill's. I got there an hour early and was happy to see Brother Paul sitting at the bar nursing a beer. In his black cape and black hat, he looked like Count Dracula.

"You had dinner yet?" I asked him.

"No," he said.

"Let's go down the street for a little chili rice," I suggested.

"Good idea."

The line was long, and when I got to the front, Chester smiled.

"Checking to see if we've heard from Vernon?" he asked.

"Haven't heard a word," said Essie, looking up from a steaming vat of chili. "It's only been a day."

"What are they talking about?" asked Brother Paul.

"I'll tell you while we eat."

We brought our chili rice back to Big Bill's and ate at the bar. I gave Brother Paul a shorthand version of Vernon's story.

"You know," he said, "I remember that song 'Faith.' They were playing it around here some time ago."

"I think I heard it too. But what about a tune called 'Willing Woman/Willing Man' and 'Leavin' Ain't the Last Thing on My Mind'?"

"Never heard 'em," said Paul. "How about you?"

"Don't know those songs."

"I'll tell you who damn sure *would* know," Paul offered.

"Who's that?"

"Ranger Roy Finkelstein."

"Who the hell is that?"

"He owns the Record Dump over in Garland. He's got every damn record that's ever been made. He's got piles of those shellacs from the old days. Boogie-woogie, Western swing, polkas—hell, there ain't nothing Ranger Roy don't carry and nothing he don't know. The man's a walking encyclopedia of music."

"How do you know him?"

"Nutsy. Him and Nutsy are partners."

"I didn't think Nutsy cared anything about music."

"He don't. Him and Ranger Roy run a bookie operation out of the back room."

"Didn't they close it down when Nutsy was busted?"

"They closed down Nutsy's Fort Worth operations. But they didn't know about Garland. No one pays attention to Garland. But Garland's where all the big action is. There's more to Garland than meets the eye."

Garland is a flat, dusty suburb on the eastern flank of Dallas. They say Garland should be renamed "Carland" because of all the used car dealers dotting the landscape. On a small side street right off Garland Avenue, sitting between a gas station and a deserted lot, I spotted a small frame house that had been converted to a store. In the window was a stenciled sign that said THE RECORD DUMP.

I arrived, alone, the very next day after Brother Paul had mentioned the place. I was eager to see whether Vernon's story could be verified.

What had been the house's living and dining rooms were filled with wooden record bins containing long-play 33⅓ rpm albums. The walls were lined with shelves that contained 45 singles, as well as 10-inch extended play records. There was a whole huge section devoted to 78s, both singles and multi-sleeved albums. The massive inventory was divided by category—country, R&B, rock and roll, show tunes, and the like. Hanging from the ceiling were colorful posters for shows, most of them from Dewey Groom's Longhorn Ballroom, a popular Dallas dance hall where you could see everyone from Ferlin Husky to B.B. King.

Sitting at a desk, his feet propped up and a slim unlit cigar hanging from his lips, was a man I presumed to be Ranger Roy Finkelstein. I say that because he was wearing a fire-engine-red sweatshirt that said SUPPORT YOUR TEXAS RANGERS OR PAY THE CONSEQUENCES. Under the words was a drawing of a smoldering pistol. On the man's head was a beat-up blue baseball cap with U.S. POST OFFICE stitched above the brim. His dark eyes popped out like a frog. His long eyebrows tilted down and met in the middle. He wasn't ugly—he had a friendly face—but you sure couldn't call him pretty. He spoke in a friendly manner.

"Can I help you with something?"

"Sure can," I said. "I'm a friend of Brother Paul."

"The drummer?"

"The same."

"You a musician?"

"Try to be."

"Got any records out there?"

"A few you probably haven't heard of."

When I mentioned them, he knew every one. He sounded pleased to meet me.

"Actually, I came over here to ask about a band. Ever heard of Good Friends?"

"Out of Round Rock, Texas," he said without a second's hesitation. "Put out a few singles and a couple of albums on Ring Dawson's little label in San Antone. Only real hit was 'Faith.' First album was called *Good Friends*, and the second was *Still Good Friends*. But by the time the second one came out, the band had busted up. Too bad. I thought they had something going."

"Ever hear 'em live?"

"I didn't. But I got copies of both albums if you wanna hear 'em."

"I do."

Ranger Roy had no trouble locating both. Each of them had pictures of the band. I was excited to actually see the characters Vernon had written about. The first thing that struck me was that on both album covers, Willard and Marla were standing in front. I knew it was Marla because Vernon had described her as

blond and busty with a button nose and dimples in her cheeks. She was definitely a fox. He'd also written that Willard was over six feet tall with blond hair and blue eyes. Well, that's just what he looked like in these two pictures. Fact is, Willard and Marla looked like a couple. On the second album cover, he even had his arm around her. The other band members pictured were in the background. Sticks was behind his drum set.

Like Vernon had written, Cynthia was certainly a "raven-haired beauty." I was especially moved to see Vernon standing up straight. With his square jaw and burning brown eyes, he stared down the camera. I could feel his steely determination. He was definitely the leader of the band, but it was clear that someone—probably Ring Dawson—had pushed the All-American-looking lead singers up front.

On the first album, they wore plain clothes. On the second, they had on Western-style costumes—jackets with fringe, and cowboy boots. Other than that, the differences between the two cover shots were slight. In both instances, the spotlight stayed on Marla and Willard.

"How much are these records?" I asked Ranger Roy.

"Oh, hell, you can have 'em both for a buck. They just been lying around here collecting dust."

I gave him a dollar and thanked him kindly.

"One more thing," I said. "You ever hear of a man named Skeeter Jarvis?"

"Knew him well. Rebuilt guitars down there in Austin. Helluva guitarist himself."

"Presume he's dead."

"Been dead for years. Crazy as a loon. You'd drop by his shop and he'd give you a private concert. You'd think you were listening to Les Paul or Chet Atkins. But then the poor son-of-a-bitch would get in front of a crowd and freeze up. His face would turn red as a tomato and he'd run off."

"I believe he had something to do with this band," I said, pointing to the two Good Friends albums.

"Could be. Couple of times I ran into him at Ring's studio in San Antone. Him and Ring were good buddies."

"Is Ring alive?"

"Alive and well. He wound up in high cotton managing Bambi Love."

"The one who sings that 'Cheatin' Ways' song they're playing on the radio?" I asked.

"*This* one," said Ranger Roy, pointing to the pictures of Marla on the cover of both albums.

"What do you mean?"

"I mean that this ol' gal, whatever her name used to be, is now Bambi Love."

"You sure?"

"As sure as a bear shits in the woods. Ever seen Bambi Love's picture?"

"Don't think so."

"Well, just take a gander."

He went to the back, where he riffled through some papers and came up with a glossy publicity photo.

"Am I right," he asked, "or am I right?"

Ranger Roy was right. Marla and Bambi were the same lady—same flowing blond hair, same emerald-green eyes, same come-hither smile. Bambi was obviously older—a woman in her mid-twenties, while Marla looked like a teenager. Bambi was also sexier.

Wearing a low-cut tight-fitting blouse, Bambi seemed especially happy to show off her big boobs.

"Quite a looker," said Roy.

Still looking at the photo, I had to agree. "You got a copy of that single?"

"Sure do. The thing's selling like hotcakes."

"Has she come out with an album?"

"Just this single. Last I heard from Ring, she's working on an album that'll be ready by spring."

"Also wondering if, by any chance, you got Ring's number?"

"He's somewhere in my Rolodex."

Ranger Roy went to an old rolltop desk piled high with papers. He spun 'round his Rolodex and stopped at the card he was looking for. He copied down the number on the receipt for the records I'd just bought.

"Last I heard, Ring's busy running 'tween San Antone and Nashville. His San Antone number's the only one I got."

"I'll give it a try," I said.

"What's your interest in all this, if I might ask?"

"Looking for a friend."

I paid for the records and was about to leave when Ranger Roy stopped me to say, "If you're a friend of Brother Paul's, might be safe to assume that you share some of his favorite pastimes."

"Such as?"

"Cards. Paul's been known to like a good game of poker, not to mention dominoes. How 'bout you?"

"I went to Baylor down in Waco for a semester, where I majored in dominoes."

Ranger Roy smiled. "Then follow me out back and let me introduce you around."

The back was a big two-car garage converted to a gaming room. There were a couple of desks where some good ol' boys were taking bets on their phones. There were also three card tables. Two were devoted to poker and one to dominoes. To make a long story short, I devoted the rest of my afternoon to testing my gambling skills. I'm pleased to say that my skills came through. I left Ranger Roy Finkelstein's enterprising establishment not only with the two Good Friends albums and the Bambi Love single, but over two hundred dollars in winnings to boot.

CHEATIN' WAYS

I said, "I'll love you, darlin'
For the rest of your days
And never go back
To my cheatin' ways"
You believed my words
My heart was true
I'd never do a thing
To ever hurt you
But then he comes along
Like a prince out of a book
And turns me around
With one long lovin' look
Wish I were stronger
And could stay away
But this man's brought out
My cheatin' ways

I was back home listening to this single by Bambi Love. It was a song that sounded more like something a man would sing than a woman. Men are known to be cheaters. Women are the ones we're cheating on. Women don't usually sing about wronging but rather about being wronged. And yet this singer—this woman with this low-toned super-sexy voice—was almost proud of her cheatin' ways. Maybe that's what made the song a hit. It was daring. And it was different.

Yet it wasn't all that different from one of the songs on *Still Good Friends* called "Cheatin' Days." Like all the tunes on the records, the writer listed was Vernon Clay. The melody was eerily similar and so was the rhythm. The only difference was the story. In "Cheatin' Days," Marla is singing about how her man comes home at night but runs around during the day. In "Cheatin' Ways," Bambi is the one running around. The writer and producer on "Cheatin' Ways" was listed as Slick Walters. Didn't know the guy, but hell, there were a lot of Nashville writers I hadn't heard of. I couldn't help but think that this writer flat-out stole Vernon's song. And I also couldn't help but wonder whether Vernon knew about it.

On the two Good Friends albums, the track I liked the most was the only one that Vernon sang—"Faith." All the others were either Marla singing alone or with

Willard. They were okay. Vernon's songs were all well crafted. The stories made sense. But the duet singing of Marla and Willard was pretty ordinary. Kinda went in one ear and out the other. Vernon, though, was a different story. He sounded for real. You knew that his feelings weren't fake. His voice was strong. It carried a cry and a plea that you couldn't ignore. Damn shame, I thought, that he didn't sing on some of those other tracks.

All this music stayed on my mind as Brother Paul and I packed up and headed down to San Antone. They call it Mission City 'cause of the old Spanish missions there. But I was seeing it as Mission City 'cause it fit my mission. San Antone was headquarters for Ring Dawson. I was sure this booking in a San Antone dance hall was proof that mysterious forces were keeping me on the path of learning more about Vernon.

Soon as I hit town, I called over to Ring's Records. I got connected to an answering service. Frustrated, I got the address out of the phone book and drove over there.

It was a little warehouse a few miles from the Alamo. It didn't look much like a studio, but hell, you can put a studio anywhere. Knocked on the door. No answer. Knocked louder. Still no answer. Maybe they were recording. This time I banged on the door with my fist.

"Ain't no one there, mister," said a man who came out of a janitorial supply store next door.

"Looking for Ring Dawson," I said.

"You missed him by a month. Ring's long gone. Shut down his operation. Moved to Nashville."

"You know where in Nashville?"

"No idea."

Dead end.

San Antone turned out to be doubly dead. Not only did I miss Dawson, I also missed getting paid after our gig. The owner slipped out before we got offstage, leaving word that he had to be in bankruptcy court the next morning. But Brother Paul wasn't buying it. He found out where the man lived and paid him a two a.m. visit. Didn't get all our money, but enough to pay for gas back to Fort Worth.

"Hell," said Brother Paul as we headed for the highway, "we got enough gas money to take us all the way to Nashville."

"You wanna go to Nashville?" I asked.

"Ain't a bad idea," he said. "You're the one who calls Nashville 'the Store.' You're always saying that if you wanna sell songs, you gotta bring 'em to the Store."

"Yup. I believe that's true."

"So it's settled."

Before I could say yes or no, Brother Paul turned on the radio. A deejay was saying, "Here's a hot one from that little lady who's burning up the airwaves with her 'Cheatin' Ways.' Here's Bambi Love."

"Maybe so," I finally said, thinking about my two-hundred-dollar poker winnings. "Maybe Nashville is the right move after all. Maybe Nashville's the place to live."

MUSIC CITY

Back in the early 1960s, Nashville was a funny place. At first glance, it seemed relaxed and laid-back. If you were a picker or songwriter, you'd find your way over to Tootsie's Orchid Lounge, across the alley from the Ryman Auditorium, where the Grand Ole Opry carried on every Saturday night. Tootsie was a sweetheart. She had a good word for all the writers, even if you were new to town like me. She made me feel welcome.

Underneath the fellowship, though, was a strong strain of killer competition. Sure, your fellow songwriter might inspire you with his latest composition. But if you were looking to get your song to a big artist, say, like Marty Robbins or Patsy Cline, he'd have no compunction about tripping you up to get to those artists before you. Nashville was tough.

To give myself time to get settled, I arrived without my family. Hard as I tried, I couldn't find steady work. There were a lot of clubs featuring live music, but there were a lot more—hundreds more—live musicians looking to get hired. When the wife and kids arrived, all I could afford was twenty-dollar-a-week accommodations in a trailer park, the same seedy one that Roger Miller would sing about in "King of the Road." Bottom line: I had to go back to hawking encyclopedias door to door.

I had one shabby dark suit, one white shirt and one red-striped tie. My black lace-up shoes had holes in the soles. This was my uniform as I hit the streets, ready but hardly eager to sell books of knowledge to the good citizens of Nashville. The sales manager gave me a list of homes to hit up, all in an area of four or five square miles.

My third day out, I still hadn't sold a thing. It was early April but still no sign of spring. Winter was hanging tough. The air was frosty cold, and without an overcoat, I was chilled to the bone. Lugging my briefcase stuffed with sales brochures and sample books, I walked up and down the tree-lined streets of a nice neighborhood of two-story houses. Knocking on the door or ringing the doorbell, I was usually greeted by either an angry dog or an angry homeowner who resented the disturbance. I didn't blame 'em.

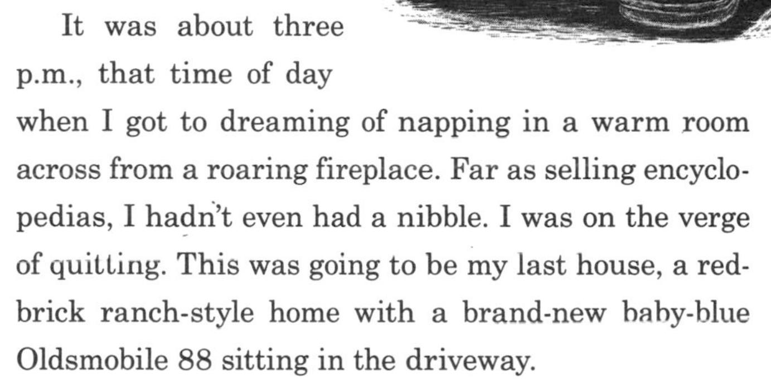

It was about three p.m., that time of day when I got to dreaming of napping in a warm room across from a roaring fireplace. Far as selling encyclopedias, I hadn't even had a nibble. I was on the verge of quitting. This was going to be my last house, a red-brick ranch-style home with a brand-new baby-blue Oldsmobile 88 sitting in the driveway.

A woman who looked to be in her late forties came to the door. She had a pretty face, a dyed red beehive hairdo high on her head, and an orange velour pantsuit. Nice figure, nice smile, seemed like a nice lady. She spoke in a thick Southern accent, saying that she and her husband had two kids in junior high, and just by coincidence, she'd been thinking how it might help their studies to have a set of encyclopedias sitting in the den. In short, this was the easiest sale of my life. No, she didn't need the easy payment plan. And yes, she could give me a check right now. She was fine with a two-week delivery time. Making out the sales slip, I asked her full name.

"Ruby Walters."

"Walters," I repeated. "Your husband isn't in the music business, is he?"

"Why, he certainly is. Jack Walters."

"Sometimes called Slick?"

"Personally, I never call him that. To me he's Jack. It's just that the music business likes to give out nicknames. But I don't think he's slick. I think he's sweet. At least he used to be."

"Is he home?" I asked. "I'd like to thank him for his business."

"You can thank me," said Ruby. "He don't care too much about books. He don't care too much about anything except his hit records. Right now he's at the studio. He practically lives there."

"If I'm not mistaken, ma'am, he wrote 'Cheatin' Ways' for Bambi Love."

"Oh, that woman . . ." said Ruby, her voice trailing off as her face flushed and her eyes narrowed.

"I'm guessing she's gonna be a big star," I said, hoping to hear more.

"If you can't say anything good about a person, don't say anything at all."

I knew I'd better drop the subject.

"Just wanna thank you again for your order, Mrs. Walters."

"Ruby," she corrected me. "Call me Ruby."

Was there something suggestive about the way she invited me to call her Ruby? Or was it just my imagination? Either way, I shook her hand, which was extremely warm, and went on my way.

Turned out to be a great day. Four doors down from Ruby, I sold a set of encyclopedias to a grandmother with instructions to send it to her son and grandkids in Memphis. Two sales in two hours—a record for me.

I decided to give up the rest of my route and go home. In driving home, though, I really wasn't thinking about encyclopedia sales. I was thinking about Vernon—thinking that, although I'd lost all track of him, I really hadn't. I was back on his tail, back on the trail that would lead me to learn more about him. And the weirdest thing—the one thing I couldn't explain—is that all this had come about without trying. Maybe there *were* unknown powers, maybe there *were* strange pockets of positive energy that were conspiring in my favor. I remembered what I'd told my Sunday school class back in Fort Worth: "I'm working on a good cause and you all have inspired me to keep at it." Maybe the universe was feeling my inspiration and doing all it could to help me out. At least it made me feel good to think so.

Don't wanna get too philosophical, but it sure does seem like the more you go with the flow, the more you get where you want to go. That was exactly the case of my early days in Nashville. In May, a small publisher had given me a steady job writing songs. This was a miracle. For the first time in my life, I was actually paid to sit in a small office and fool with my guitar until I came up with a decent tune or two. Not only did this mean I could quit the door-to-door encyclopedia routine, I had a legitimate reason to seek out Slick Walters: I had songs to sell.

"I don't believe Walters is too interested in anyone's songs but his own," said Brother Paul when I told him that I was about to make my move. On weekends, I'd put together a band where Brother Paul, myself, a bass player and a steel guitarist were working clubs around the city.

"Well, Slick does more than write," I said. "He's also a producer. That means he has artists who need hit songs. He can't possibly write all of 'em."

"He can try."

"You ever meet the man?" I asked Paul.

"No, but I hear he's a prick."

"Says who?"

"Says Jimmy Dale, a buddy of mine, a drummer who's been working on his dates. Says that he found a way to screw Ring Dawson . . ."

"The record man from San Antone who moved here . . ."

"And now's moved back to San Antone 'cause Slick done pulled one of his slick moves and pushed Ring out of the picture. Now Slick's doing more than writing and producing for Bambi Love. Now he's managing her."

"I gotta meet this man."

"If you do, I'm tagging along," said Paul.

"You don't need to bother."

"The hell I don't. Jimmy Dale says he packs heat and got a nasty temper to boot. You never know what the hell he's gonna do."

"I got no reason to piss him off," I said.

"You sure about that?"

"Well, not entirely."

A couple of days later, Brother Paul and I were walking into a small one-story building on Division Street, just around the corner from Nashville's Music Row. The sign outside said WALTERS ENTERTAINMENT PRODUCTS, JACK WALTERS, PROPRIETOR. A middle-aged woman with a long face and tired eyes asked our business.

"We're friends of Jimmy Dale, the drummer," said Paul. "He said it'd be okay if we came by the session today."

"Mr. Walters's sessions are closed," she instructed us.

"Oh, it's okay, Margaret," said Jimmy, who walked through the front door. "These are my pals. Come on back, fellas."

Paul introduced me to Jimmy, a portly man in his early forties, of good cheer and bouncy energy.

"Hear you got a couple of hit songs out there," Jimmy said to me. "Got something to play for Slick?"

"That's why I brought my guitar," I said.

"Good deal. Slick's always hungry for hits. Like I told Paul, he'll be glad to meet you."

We walked down a long hallway leading to the recording studio. The walls were covered with show posters of country artists Slick produced. None of them were superstars, but I recognized several as having current popular songs. The picture that caught my eye was a framed advertisement for Bambi Love's "Cheatin' Ways" in *Cash Box*, the trade magazine. "Smash hit of the year!" the ad declared. The photo of

Bambi was from the waist up. She wore a white sweater tight enough to grab my attention.

Jimmy noticed me noticing Bambi.

"We're almost done with her album," he said. "We're cutting the last song today."

"What's it been like working with her?" I asked.

"What I can say? She's a fox."

Just by chance, I knew all three of the musicians who were in the studio. Two were from Texas and the third I'd met at Tootsie's. Handshakes all around.

"Slick's back in his office," said Jimmy. "He'll be coming out soon. And Bambi, hell, you never know when she'll show up. She wanders in whenever she feels like it."

I shot the shit with the musicians for the next thirty minutes until the studio door opened and a man wearing a shiny jet-black toupee stormed through. The toupee was the first thing I noticed. It was that obvious. The wig was fashioned into a sharp wave that, jutting out a couple of inches past his forehead, had the same shape as the fancy fin taillights on a '61 Cadillac DeVille. The toupee seemed to have a life of its own. I half expected the thing to fly off his head and zoom around the room. Beneath the wig were a set of intense gray eyes, large ears, a long nose and thin lips on a mouth fixed in a scowl. The man was medium height and medium build. He wore a black Western shirt with white stitching, and blue jeans held up by a belt and a buckle with his oversized initials—JW—in brass. His face looked a good twenty years older than his wig. I guessed he was in his fifties.

"Slick," said Jimmy. "Meet a couple of pals."

Jimmy introduced Paul and me.

"I see you got your guitar with you," Slick said in a bottom-of-the-barrel baritone voice. "You looking to play on this session?"

"I was actually looking to play you a couple of songs of mine," I said.

"Had any hits?"

When I named a couple, he said, "Hell, I didn't know you wrote those. Sure, I'll listen to your songs, but first take out your guitar. Last night I wrote a song myself. There's a guitar solo after the first verse. You might want to take a crack at it."

"Sure thing."

In spite of all the warnings, Slick acted like a pretty normal guy. Hell, he was willing to hear my songs and invited me to play on his session. He didn't seem crazy at all.

"Lemme show you this new song," he said.

Slick wasn't a musician, so he couldn't play the tune on any instrument. He also explained that, because he couldn't read music, no notes were written down. All he had was a yellow pad with lyrics. He put the pad on a stand and, before he started singing, said, "I got a low voice, and this thing is written for Bambi. You're gonna have to close your eyes and imagine her singing it."

Easier said than done.

In his froglike voice, Slick sang a song called "Something I Got." It was an up-tempo tune that sounded awfully familiar. The story was written from a woman's point of view. *"Early in the morning or in the midnight hour . . . something I got gives me all the power . . ."*

When he was through singing, he told Jimmy Dale to lay down a beat. He pointed to the piano player to work up some chords. The bass player fell right in. Thanks to the professionalism of these musicians, the song came together quickly. After they ran it down once, Slick showed me where he wanted a guitar solo. No problem.

But then something funny happened. While playing the solo, I suddenly realized why the song sounded familiar. It was basically a rewrite of Vernon Clay's "Something You Got," the tune that was supposed to be the A side until "Faith," the B side, took off instead. Not only was "Something You Got" released as a single, it also appeared on Good Friends' first album that, by now, I'd listened to many times. Just as Slick had ripped off Vernon's "Cheatin' Days" and turned it into "Cheatin' Ways," he was now turning "Something You Got" into "Something I Got." None of this was sitting well with me.

"Beautiful," said Slick when my solo was over. "Now let's run through the whole thing again so when Bambi shows up, we can knock it out in a just a couple of takes."

"One quick question, Slick," I said.

"Shoot," he urged.

"I'm presuming you've heard all those records Bambi made when she sang with Good Friends."

When I said that, I was sitting down and Slick was standing over me. His expression changed. His mouth tightened and his eyes reddened.

He practically spit out the words, "What the hell does that have to do with anything?"

"Well, the guy who put the band together, Vernon Clay—"

"Never heard of him," Slick interrupted.

"Anyway, he's the one who wrote 'Something You

Got.' It was their first single. Bambi, who was calling herself Marla back then, she sang it and—"

"What the hell you babbling about?" Slick interrupted me again. "I ain't got time for no stories. We're here to make a record."

"Well, that's just my point," I said. "She already made the record. Vernon called it 'Something You Got,' and the one you just showed us—except for changing the 'you' to 'I'—is basically the same song."

Reacting to my words, Brother Paul and Jimmy tensed up. My frankness surprised them.

Slick leaned down and got right in my face. I could smell his bad breath. I could practically see flames shooting out of his eyes.

"Son-of-a-bitch," he said, "you calling me a thief?"

"I'm just calling Vernon Clay a damn good writer."

"I never even heard of that bastard."

"Maybe not, but you sure as hell must have heard his song."

"What gives you the damn right to walk into another man's studio—a studio I paid for with my own sweat, a studio built on my hit records that I produced? Where do you come off waltzing in here and accusing me of stealing some song from a man I don't know from Adam?"

"You don't have to know him," I said. "You just have to know his song. Just the way, I suspect, you knew Bambi Love's 'Cheatin' Ways.' That's a tune that came out under your name but was originally written by Vernon Clay, who called it 'Cheatin' Days.'"

That did it. Slick exploded. He grabbed me by my neck. I reacted by kicking him in the nuts. He moaned, releasing his grip on me and nearly falling over. But before he hit the floor, he got control of himself and ran out of the studio.

"Let's get the hell outta here," said Brother Paul.

I agreed, but before we could, Slick was back in the room holding a pistol aimed dead at my head. My life suddenly flashed before me.

Because Slick was focused on me, he didn't see Paul reach for his piece. Neither did I. I didn't understand what was happening until I heard Paul say, "Put it down, Slick, before I blow your ugly mug to smithereens."

No one in the room could question Paul's intent. Paul was just as crazy as Slick—maybe crazier—and Slick, though still fuming, came to reason.

"If either one of you cocksuckers gets within ten feet of my studio, I swear I'll kill you," he said as me and Paul—still pointing his gun at Slick—backed out of the room.

Once outside, Paul was shaking his head. "Didn't I warn you?"

"You sure did."

"Then what the hell were you doing back there?" he asked.

"Just looking for some answers."

"Yeah, but in all the wrong places."

"Sometimes you gotta go to the wrong place to get the right answer," I said.

"I don't know about that. All I know is that I need a drink."

"The drinks are on me, buddy," I said. "That's the least I can do."

MAN WITH A MONOCLE

Two things I love about Memphis, Tennessee: The first is how the fragrance of sweet barbecue is always in the air. And the second is the Peabody Hotel, where every day at eleven in the morning the elevator opens and a line of five trained ducks files out to the tune of "King Cotton March" and waddle over to splash in the elaborate fountain that sits in the middle of the lobby.

I wasn't staying at the Peabody—Howard Johnson was more my speed—but a promoter who'd heard me and my band at a Beale Street club invited me over there for a late breakfast.

Experience has taught me to view promoters skeptically. They're big talkers with big plans who sometimes turn out to be big thieves. This particular promoter, Geoffrey Jerguson, intrigued me 'cause he wore a monocle, dressed in wool tweeds in mid-May and spoke with a British accent. He wanted to impress me with all the big shots he knew in the music business. He loved to gossip. He claimed to be friends with Colonel Parker, Elvis's manager. He claimed to be friends with everyone.

When I arrived at the Peabody, the lobby was lined with tourists on two sides, clearing a pathway for the mallards that were exiting the elevator and heading for the fountain. As the ducks were quacking, children were squealing with delight. Looking over the crowd, on the other side of the lobby I noticed a sexy lady in a short black leather skirt. Her breasts were practically busting out of her form-fitting green blouse. Her hair was curly blond, her lipstick the color of fresh blood. Damn if it wasn't Marla! It was Bambi Love!

"Miss Love!" I hollered.

I don't know if she heard me, but at the very minute I moved to approach her, the ducks had started their march. I couldn't risk stepping on one of those creatures, so I had to wait till they waddled by. Unexpectedly, one of the ducks turned around and headed back to the elevator. Their trainer, the Duck Master, had to correct the fowl's course and point the little guy back to the fountain. This took a minute or two.

By the time I could get to the other side of the lobby, Bambi was gone. I went out on the street, looked in every direction, but no sign of her. Back inside, I asked the clerk behind the desk whether a Bambi Love was registered at the hotel.

"She just checked out," said the clerk.

"If you are inquiring about the charming Miss Love, I can tell you all you want to know," said Geoffrey Jerguson, who happened to be standing next to me and overheard my question.

"How do you know her?"

"I'm promoting her in England."

"I'd like to hear more about her," I said.

"And you will. Let's proceed to the dining room for tea and crumpets."

"Or bourbon and barbecue. This is Memphis."

"Indeed."

Turned out I had corned beef hash and Jerguson had a mushroom omelet.

"They like country music in England?" I asked.

"We adore it. As we speak, Roy Orbison is out touring with the Beatles all over the U.K."

I had heard some Beatles songs. They hadn't been

to America yet, so I didn't even know what they looked like. But I did know that Roy Orbison had heard my demo of "Pretty Paper" and was considering singing it. I couldn't have been happier. Roy Orbison was a great singer and big star. But with this strange Englishman sitting across from me, I really wanted to hear about Bambi Love.

"When did you first hear Bambi?" I asked him.

"Same time you did, I presume. The single. 'Cheatin' Ways.' When it reached number one, I recalled how, some years back, Teresa Brewer, another American female country singer, was very big in Britain. I immediately saw the same possibility for Bambi. So I booked a flight and came to see this chap called Slick."

"What'd you think of him?"

"The name fits him rather well."

I didn't mention my run-in with Slick last month in Nashville. What would be the point?

"I was hardly surprised to see that Slick's involvement in Miss Love's life involves far more than producing and managing her," said Jerguson.

"Why do you say that?"

"For the past few nights they have been sharing the presidential suite of this very hotel. When they invited me up last night for cocktails, they were quite cozy with one another."

"Is Slick still here?" I asked, wondering if the madman might be stalking the lobby.

"No. He went back to Nashville early this morning and will meet Miss Love later in the week in Atlanta."

"What were they doing in Memphis?"

"They suggested I meet them here rather than Nashville. Slick said he'd promised his star a little getaway, a celebration for the great success of her newly released album."

"I didn't know it was out."

"I happen to have a copy in hand." And with that, he reached down into his oversized case and fished out a copy of the LP. No doubt about it, the cover shot was a stunner: Bambi in a let-it-all-hang-out scarlet-red dress. She was all smiles and, for obvious reasons, shot from the side. I stared longer than I needed to. I flipped it over and saw that the credits read, "Produced by Jack Walters. All songs written by Jack Walters."

"But enough about Miss Love," said Jerguson. "Let's talk about you and the delightful prospects of introducing you to a world of potential fans across the pond."

For the next half hour, Geoffrey Jerguson talked about Club Mustang, a nightspot that he and some other fellow were opening in London. The idea was to bring over American country-and-western artists. While I was pretty well known in Texas and was building a reputation in other parts of the country, I'd hardly call myself a star. It was hard to believe that I could draw much of a crowd in England.

"Some of your songs are big hits over there," said Jerguson.

"Songs sung by other artists," I reminded him. "Ferlin Husky, Ray Price, Patsy Cline. Those are the artists you should be booking."

"They're a bit out of my price range."

"But no one's heard of me in England."

"I can stimulate interest. I can garner press coverage."

"When are you thinking about?"

"Miss Bambi Love will facilitate our grand opening the second week of June. We'd like you to follow her."

Why not? I figured. *What did I have to lose?*

When we started talking turkey, the deal became even more attractive. His offer was exactly double of what we'd been getting playing dance halls in Texas and Tennessee. He sealed the deal when he said, "Given your great curiosity about Bambi, I'd be delighted to fly you over a day early so you can catch her last show."

PRETTY PAPER

I should have seen it coming when we were booked on a fly-by-night, no-frills, no-food airline with a six-hour stopover in Reykjavík, Iceland. When we finally arrived in London, there was no one to greet us. So we took a cab to the address on our itinerary, which turned out to be a fleabag hotel across the street from a burnt-out warehouse. Starving and jet-lagged, I fell asleep for twelve straight hours.

When I woke up, it was Saturday morning. That night was Bambi Love's last show at Club Mustang. I planned to arrive early and finally have a chance to ask her some questions. My band didn't open till Monday, so there was time to recuperate from the long flight. Our other two bandmates were still sleeping when Brother Paul and I went out to grab some grub at a corner café. We were both glad to see ham and eggs on the menu.

I happened to look down and on the floor saw a copy of the *Daily Mail*, one of those splashy English tabloids. I don't know what made me pick it up, but I did. The big news was how the old minister of finance was caught pants-down with a young high-priced hooker. As I turned the pages, seemed like it was nothing but scandals. I was about to give up on British journalism when I came to a story that stopped me cold.

"CHEATIN' WAYS" MANAGER ATTACKS LOCAL PROMOTER FOR CHEATING

In an instance of life imitating art, the manager of American country-and-western singer Bambi Love assaulted British promoter Geoffrey Jerguson, proprietor of Club Mustang, the West End nightery where Miss Love has been performing. Her song, "Cheatin' Ways," is currently number one on Melody Maker's list of country-and-western hits.

The manager, Jack "Slick" Walters, being held by London police, told a reporter, "Jerguson is a slimeball huckster who promised us payment in advance but never came up with a plug nickel. If this is how you Brits do business, I say shame on the lot of you, and that includes your queen."

Mr. Jerguson was taken to St. Bartholomew's Hospital where, according to a spokesman, he is suffering from a concussion.

Said an eyewitness at the scene, "The crowd was whistling and stomping because the singer was two hours late coming out. Then off to the side of the stage, right where I'm standing, some lout goes after this gent wearing a monocle. He starts choking the gent and beating his head against the wall. The lout doing the beating is pounding so hard that a black wig flies right off his head. It would be funny, except for the poor gent, who'd be dead if me and some others hadn't pulled the lout off him."

A publicist for Club Mustang said the club, which opened only a fortnight ago, will be closed until further notice.

WARM TEXAS NIGHT

The comforts of home are great. Texas is my home, and it's always a comfort to return there, especially after getting burned so bad in Merrye Olde England. Texas promoters might not be a hundred percent honest, but compared to Geoffrey Jerguson, they're saints. My ol' pal Crash Stewart had lined up a bunch of dates for us all around the state, keeping me busy with one-nighters from July through October.

I'd left London with a bad attitude. I'd actually gone by the hospital where Jerguson was laid up with the idea of maybe, just maybe, getting some money out of the man. Turned out, though, that Slick had broken his jaw. Jerguson couldn't speak. And even if he could, what was he gonna tell me? It was a lost cause.

I wondered what had happened to Bambi. With Slick in jail, where had she gone? I considered trying to find her, but by then I was fed up with the chase. What was the point? My so-called mission—of getting to the bottom of Vernon's story and helping him out—had led to a dead end. If I hadn't been so distracted by my mission, I would have seen through Jerguson's bullshit and never left the country. My mission was clouding my judgment and keeping me from seeing people for who they really were. Slick, Jerguson, Marla-Bambi—the whole lot of them were no good. Liars and scammers, they used each other and anyone else they could con. Their enterprise was corrupt to the core. Thinking I was onto something, believing I could make a difference, all I'd done was chase my own tail. It was about time to face the truth—I'd been a fool.

When there was a problem with our return plane tickets, I had to call my Nashville publisher to wire me money. That was the last straw. Now Vernon Clay and the mysteries surrounding him were officially part of my past.

My present was this long trek through Texas. I'd started out in Houston and worked my way up the state to Waco and Dallas and was now playing the

Stagecoach Ballroom in Fort Worth, one of the bigger venues for live music in the city, where it was nice to see that I could still draw a crowd.

After the big Saturday-night show, I was glad to see Big Bill come up to the bandstand to say hello.

"Who's tending bar?" I asked him as I leaned over to shake his hand.

"Couldn't miss your show, ol' buddy," he said. "Glad to see you've come up in the world."

"Not as far up as you'd think. Still singing for my supper."

"You around tomorrow?" asked Bill.

"Yes, sir. We don't head out for Wichita Falls till Monday."

"Well, come by tomorrow night. I'll buy you a drink and some of that chili rice you're so crazy about."

"You got a deal."

Didn't think that much about it. It was always fun to shoot the shit with Big Bill. And I could practically taste that chili rice. Be nice to say hello to Chester and Essie.

I have to confess that Vernon Clay did enter my mind. Maybe he'd moved back in. Maybe they knew his whereabouts. Maybe . . . but no, I was through chasing down Vernon. Just give me some chili rice.

We'd forgotten that Chester and Essie were closed on Sunday. So much the better. It was enough to sit with Big Bill, who grilled up a couple of burgers, and hear the local scuttlebutt. Nutsy Perkins, cleared of all charges, was back on the street and stronger than ever. Him and Ranger Roy Finkelstein were now headquartered in Denton, a little college town just north of Fort Worth, and had expanded their burgeoning bookie operation to Arkansas and Oklahoma. As for Barbara Lou, the cutie who had her eye on me, she'd finally left her old man and found work at a beauty shop just around the corner. Did I want the address?

"Better not," I said. "I got enough problems in that area."

"Care to explain?" asked Big Bill.

"Rather not."

"Enough said."

Heading back to my hotel, I left Big Bill's with a slight beer buzz. It was a warm Texas night. A yellow moon hung low in the sky. Crickets were making a racket. A mutt was chasing a black cat down an alleyway. Someone's radio was blasting Johnny Cash's "Ring of Fire." Seeing that the lights were out at the Chili Rice emporium, I walked on by. In the distance, walking toward me, was a black woman carrying a big shopping bag. When she got up close, I saw it was Essie.

"Well, I'll be," she said with a big warm smile, "just the man I been looking for. I called you, but that number you gave was no good."

"We moved to Nashville a few months back. Let me help you with that bag."

"Don't mind if you do. Just came from my sister's. She helps me grate the cheese and grind the meat for the coming week. Come on in. I got something for you."

"Seen Vernon?" I couldn't help but ask.

"Haven't seen him, but we heard from him."

We went around back to the outside staircase that led up to their above-the-store apartment.

"Look who I got with me," Essie told Chester, who was sitting next to the radio listening to a baseball game.

Chester greeted me warmly before asking, "You come to get your package?"

"I just bumped into him on the street," said Essie. "He don't know nothing 'bout that package."

"What package?" I asked.

"That one," said Essie, pointing to a stack of paper on the kitchen table.

I walked over and recognized the same multicolored paper stock Vernon had used in the first batch I'd read. I took a quick glance and saw that it was his handwriting.

"Came in the mail," said Essie. "The note said that you'd probably be coming by, and when you did, this is yours to read."

"Was there a return address?" I asked.

"Nope."

"What else did the note say?"

"Only that he was missing me and Chester, but not to worry about him."

"Well, are you gonna read it?" asked Chester.

"You bet," I said. "Gonna read it tonight."

The Western Hotel had seen better days, but the price was right and the electricity worked. I sank into a saggy easy chair that faced the window. Eerily, the window looked out on Leonards. That big ol' department store was sitting there, right across the street. I could see the exact spot where I first encountered Vernon last winter.

The floor lamp next to my chair held a dim bulb that cast a pale yellow glow on the paper in my hand. My eyes glued on the words before me, I picked up the first page and didn't stop reading until the last . . .

I left off with bright yellow paper and I'm starting off with bright yellow 'cause yellow's the color of the sun. Skeeter used to say, "Every time the sun comes up, you got reason to be hopeful. Another day, another song."

I stopped writing my story when Skeeter had taught me his "Easygoing" song 'cause I wanted to end on an upbeat note. The whole point of writing was to lift my spirits and sing my blues away. I wanted to leave off when my attitude had turned from sad to glad and I felt I had a reason to live.

Well, that might have been the happy ending of that chapter, but there were other chapters that weren't very happy. I thought I didn't need to write about those chapters. I thought I could forget them. During the day, I could beat back those memories. But when I fell asleep, the nightmares were always there. The memories became the nightmares. Now I want the nightmares to stop. And I figure the only way to do that is to write out the rest of my story.

This is light blue paper, not dark blue, 'cause even though I was still down after losing Marla, my mood wasn't completely dark. I found a way to keep going.

I moved back home to Round Rock, where I was known as Joy Goodson's grandson. In Round Rock there were folks who cared about me. Two of those folks—Meg and Tom Newberry—were friends of my grandmother's. They were good people who'd known me my whole life. They owned a small building that housed their antiques store on East Austin Avenue. They said I could stay in the apartment above the building until I got back on my feet. God bless Meg and Tom. For the first week or so, I hardly went out. I had my guitar and kept playing Skeeter's "Easygoing" over and over again. I do believe that song got me through the worst of it.

One Sunday morning, Meg and Tom asked me to go to church with them, the same church that

Grandma had attended. I wasn't all that eager to go, but, given the Newberrys' generosity, how could I refuse?

I don't know whether Reverend Olan had been told about my circumstances, but his sermon seemed directed right at me. The topic was "Overcoming Misfortunes." He said that misfortunes are temporary. You get past them by turning lemons into lemonade. I could have easily written that off as a cliché, except that Grandma was always saying that very same thing. Sitting in church, I felt closer to my grandmother than I had since she'd passed that Christmastime. Now I was glad to be there.

The gladness didn't last long, though. When we stood to sing the closing hymn, I felt heat on the back of my neck, as though someone was staring at me. I turned around and, two pews back, I saw Cynthia Simone. Our eyes met. She offered me a small smile and I tried to smile back.

After the service, I walked out with Meg and Tom. Cynthia was waiting. She was with Ryan Smith, a guy we'd gone to high school with, her big sister, Jill, and her mother, Virginia.

"I didn't know you were back, Vernon," said Cynthia.

"Just kinda passing through," I said.

"You remember Ryan, don't you?"

"Sure. Hey, Ryan."

"And my mother."

"Hello, Mrs. Simone."

"Hello, Vernon. I'm glad you're back home." I was surprised at the kindness in Mrs. Simone's greeting. I thought she'd still be angry about how Cynthia had once joined my band.

"Ryan and I are engaged," Cynthia was quick to say.

"Oh, well . . . congratulations."

"I've taken over my dad's Ford dealership," said Ryan. "We're looking for a salesman on the used car lot, just in case you're looking for work."

"Thanks," I said, "but I don't think I'd be too good at that."

"I'm not so sure," said Cynthia. "You've always had a great personality, Vernon. Everyone likes you. And given the tough times we've both gone through with those horrible people and that crazy music business, maybe this is just what you need. Something to bring you back to earth."

"I'm grateful for the offer," I said. "I really am."

"I work there, I'm the office manager," said Jill, in a sweet and alluring voice. I'd met Jill before but really didn't know her. She was older than Cynthia by two years and, at least to my eyes, much prettier. Her long brown hair was straight and shiny and fell practically to her waist. She had big bright eyes and a cute little nose. She was petite—no taller than five-foot-five—with a slender, well-proportioned figure. When she smiled, her whole face lit up. She had a sunshiny disposition that was hard to ignore.

"Well, think about it," said Ryan. "I'm there all day, every day."

"I do hope you come by, Vernon," said Jill. "Whenever my sister talked about the nightmare she went through with the band, you were the only one she said nice things about."

"I was lucky, I got out in time," said Cynthia, "but you didn't deserve what you got. You deserve better."

That night I thought about what Cynthia had said. Maybe I did deserve better. Maybe I needed to forget this music thing—at least for a while—and try something else. My savings were slowly dwindling and I couldn't live on the kindness of Meg and Tom forever. Besides, I was tired of feeling sorry for myself. Self-pity was getting me nowhere. Bottom line: I needed a job.

Pink paper 'cause I woke up early Monday morning in time to see the sunrise light the sky a soft shade of pink. I put on the only suit I owned, the one Grandma bought me for my high school graduation, and drove out to see Ryan Smith.

Smith's Round Rock Ford dealership was a big operation. New cars were sold in the main showroom flanked by a big service center on one side and a two-acre used car lot on the other. I found Ryan sitting in his office in the showroom.

"Hey, Vernon," he said, "glad to see you, buddy. You didn't have to dress up in a suit."

"Figured if I'm applying for a job . . ."

"Hell, man, you got the job. Our used car salesman showed up drunk and we fired him. You're right on time."

"You're gonna have to show me the ropes."

"Selling is easy. The key is sincerity. And I sincerely gotta tell you, man, how much I hate that prick Willard. I hated him back in high school, I hated him when he pulled the wool over Cynthia's eyes, and I hated him for what he did to you. That's why I'm happy to help you out. Any enemy of Willard's is a friend of mine."

Gaining Ryan's goodwill just because I'd been screwed over by Willard felt strange. But who was I to argue? I hardly had any qualifications and was lucky to be offered a job.

Ryan spent that first morning with me on the lot,

going over the inventory of used cars and trucks. He pointed out which vehicles represented the biggest profits and how all the prices were marked twenty-five percent higher than he'd be willing to take.

"That leaves lots of room for you to negotiate," he said. "I'm sure you're a good negotiator."

Actually I wasn't. When my first customer showed interest in a used pickup priced at four hundred dollars but then hesitated, I immediately blurted out, "You can have it for three twenty."

"All I got is two hundred bucks."

"Let me see if my boss will take that."

Ryan wasn't thrilled. "That's fifty percent off, not twenty-five."

"I know," I said, "but that's all he's got."

"He can pay more. Customers can always pay more. Tell him three hundred."

I told him and he walked. By the end of the day, I'd fumbled two other negotiations.

I was leaving the lot just when Jill was leaving the showroom.

"You look down," she said.

"I struck out," I admitted.

"This was your first day. First days don't count. You're just getting used to it."

"Not sure I ever will."

“You hungry?”

Her question took me by surprise. “Well . . .”

“I take that as a yes. I’m cooking dinner for my kid. And I always cook too much.”

“I didn’t know you had a kid. Didn’t know you were married.”

“I’m not. Truth is, we don’t really know anything about each other, do we?”

“You know about Marla . . .”

“Marla’s a bitch. Anyone could have told you that. But you look for the good in people. You’re a trusting soul, and that can be a problem. So how ’bout it—do you trust my cooking or not?”

I had to say that I did.

Purple paper, ’cause purple reminds me of pain. Jill’s interest in me, kind as it was, had me thinking of the last woman who was supposedly interested in me, the woman who was still officially my wife.

I went back to my place above the Newberrys’ store to shower and change. I was beat. The tension and frustration of the day had gotten to me. I really didn’t want to go over to Jill’s. Accepting her invitation had been a mistake. I wasn’t ready to spend time with a woman. Jill said I was a trusting person. Well, maybe. But when it came to females, my trust had been smashed to pieces. Jill was pretty. Hell, she was beautiful. But the way she came on so strong reminded me of Marla. No, going there was a bad idea. I decided to call her and tell her that, but looking at the slip of paper she'd given me, I saw an address but no phone number. I'd have to tell her in person.

I put on Levi's, a T-shirt and sneakers and drove over. She lived in a tiny wooden house on a lonely farm road only a few miles from where I'd grown up at Grandma's. When I knocked at the door, my speech was all prepared: "I'm really sorry," I was going to say, "but this isn't a great idea. Hope you haven't gone to too much trouble."

When the door opened, though, I didn't see Jill standing there. I saw a little girl holding a puppy in her arms.

"This is Toby," she said. "Toby's a boy. You want to hold him?"

"Well . . ."

"He won't bite. He's nice. He's still a baby."

Toby was a small ball of white fluff. I held him up to my face. As I looked into his dark eyes, he licked my nose.

“He’s kissing you,” said the little girl. “That’s how puppies kiss.”

“Vicky!” shouted Jill from somewhere inside the house. “Did you invite Vernon in?”

“Toby kissed him, Toby likes him.”

“Everyone likes Vernon. Have you introduced yourself?”

“I’m Vicky.”

“Nice to meet you, Vicky,” I said.

“Mama’s in the kitchen. She’s making chili rice. She only makes chili rice on special nights.”

“I sure can smell the chili,” I said.

The aroma was overwhelming. Naturally it brought back memories of Grandma.

“I actually got this recipe from your grandmother,” said Jill, who was standing over the stove and stirring the pot. She was wearing black jeans and a thin black sweater that showed off her figure. “I knew she’d won first prize at the county fair. Her chili rice is legendary around here. So one day I asked her if she’d share her secret. She not only shared it, she came over and took me through the process, step by step. Hope it measures up.”

“Wow” was all I could say. Thoughts of turning around and leaving had vanished.

"Do you want to play with me and Toby out in the yard?" asked Vicky.

"Sure," I said. "You go ahead. I'll be right there."

Vicky ran outside, with Toby scampering behind.

"Vicky's six going on sixteen," said Jill. "She stopped watching *The Mickey Mouse Club* on TV 'cause she said it was too silly. Now she watches *Father Knows Best* and keeps asking where's her father."

"Sounds like a reasonable question," I said.

"He was not a reasonable man. That's why I never married him. And that's why when he learned I was pregnant, he ran off and joined the navy. Haven't heard from him since."

"You had to be young when Vicky was born."

"Too young. Still a teenager."

"Well, you have Vicky," I said. "And she's a little sweetheart."

"Vicky makes it all worthwhile. Whatever bad thoughts I have about her dad, they go away when she looks up at me with that smile of hers."

"Mommy!" Vicky ran in the house crying. "Toby's run away."

"Vernon, can you chase after the puppy? I'm still cooking."

The backyard was enclosed by a short rickety

wooden fence with holes at the bottom big enough for a puppy to slip through.

"He ran that way," said Vicky, pointing to one of the holes.

I leaped over the fence into a wide woodsy expanse. The damn dog could be anywhere. Fortunately, a full moon provided some light, but all I could do was call out the dog's name and hope for the best. On the other side of the fence I heard Vicky crying.

I started surveying the area when I heard the howl of a coyote. My heartbeat quickened. I had to get to the puppy before the coyote did. I started calling out louder and louder. The more time passed, the more desperate I became. I started running—first this way, then that way. I was running in circles when I tripped over a fallen log and, flat on my face, heard a yelp. Inches away from me I saw these little beady eyes staring out from behind a bush. It was Toby. "Come here, boy," I said. Toby ran over to me, licked my nose and turned over on his back for a belly rub.

When I returned to the house with Toby in my arms, Vicky embraced me. Her eyes were filled with tears of joy.

"You're gonna have to keep Toby inside until someone wires over those holes in the fence," I said.

“I should have done that already,” said Jill.

“Maybe Vernon can do it,” Vicky suggested.

“No problem,” I said.

“Now that you’ve won over my daughter’s heart,” said Jill, “let’s see how my chili rice measures up to your grandmother’s.”

It measured up. The white rice had just the right texture. The salsa had just the right kick. When Jill placed a slab of melting butter on the rice before sprinkling on the chopped onions and freshly grated cheese, I couldn’t help but break into a big smile.

“You haven’t even tasted it yet,” said Jill.

I took a bite. My mouth had never been happier.

“Oh, boy” was all I said.

“Presume that means I got it right.”

“You sure did.”

During dinner, it was Vicky who did most of the talking. She brought out her dolls and told me each of their names. She showed me the drawings she had made at school. She asked whether I’d watch her dance with her Hula-Hoop.

“You bet,” I said.

“After dinner, Vicky,” said her mother.

“Do you like Elvis?” Vicky asked.

“Everyone likes Elvis,” I said.

"Good. Let's listen to Elvis records."

"Vernon's a singer," said Jill. "Wouldn't you'd rather hear him sing for us?"

"Yes!" Vicky exclaimed.

"Don't have my guitar," I said.

"Use mine," said Jill.

"Didn't know you played," I said.

"I fool with it. Don't know much except some real basic stuff. Like Jimmy Reed."

"I love Jimmy Reed," I said.

"I'll fetch the guitar."

Maybe it was the fact that I'd found Toby. Maybe it was 'cause the chili rice was so delicious. Maybe it was Vicky's sweet disposition. For whatever reasons, I was in a great mood. I took Jill's acoustic guitar and, sitting down on the couch, I played "Faith," the song inspired by my grandmother. Jill was next to me. Vicky was seated on the floor at my feet.

"I like that," said Vicky, looking up at me. "Can you sing any other songs?"

"Sure thing."

As I sang a couple of songs, Vicky never took her eyes off me.

"Okay, sweetheart," said Jill after my third song, "time to turn in. You get one story and that's it."

"Can Vernon tell me a story?"

"Not sure I know any," I admitted.

"Well, you sure know songs," said Vicky.

"Can Vernon sing me another song, Mommy?"

"You're wearing him out, Vicky."

"I don't mind," I said.

Pink paper 'cause Vicky's bedroom was painted pink. Her blanket was pink, with drawings of blue and gold angels.

I sat at the edge of her bed. Toby leaped up and sat on my lap. The song I sang Vicky was the lullaby my grandmother had taught me as a child.

All night, all day,
Angels watching over me, oh Lord
All night, all day,
Angels watching over me

Sun is setting in the west
Angels watching over me, oh Lord
Sleep my child, take your rest
Angels watching over me

Now I lay me down to sleep
Angels watching over me, oh Lord

I pray the Lord my soul to keep

Angels watching over me

When I was through, Vicky reached out to me with open arms. She hugged me tight and said, "Will you come back tomorrow?"

"I'm not sure about that."

"I'll get Mommy to invite you."

"Go to sleep, sweetheart," said Jill, tucking her in and kissing her good night.

Jill and I went back to the kitchen, where she said, "Looks like you made a friend."

"What can I say?"

"You can say whether you want a cup of coffee or something stronger."

"Coffee's fine."

While Jill made coffee, I sat back down on the couch and softly strummed her guitar.

"Cream and sugar?" she asked.

"Just black."

She placed the mug of coffee on an end table and sat next to me. She was close enough to where our knees touched. That made me uncomfortable.

"Can I make a confession?" she asked.

"Not sure how to answer that."

"Well, I'll confess anyway. When Cynthia was

going with Willard and joined your band, I used to come to your shows. I used to stand there and think, *Wow, Vernon Clay is not only a cool-looking guy, he's a damn great guitarist.* I was always waiting for you to sing, but Willard and that Marla did most of the singing. I always wondered why."

"I liked being in the background," I admitted.

"How come?"

"It's where I could focus on the guitar."

"But on that first record, that song you sang for us tonight, you did the singing. You sang 'Faith.'"

"Well, that was different."

"It was also a hit, wasn't it? At least around here they were playing it on the radio all the time."

"It did pretty good."

"But it didn't prove to you that you should sing?"

"Back then I wasn't really thinking about singing. I'm still not."

"How 'bout if I gave you something to sing?"

"What do you mean?" I asked.

"The thing is, Vernon, I'm a bookkeeper by day and a poet by night. I've always written poems, ever since I was a little girl. Some of them sound like songs to me, but I can't sing and can barely play this guitar. Maybe you can hear a melody in these poems. What do you say?"

If I told the truth, I would have said that I wanted to leave. The more intimate things got, the more uncomfortable I felt. The way Jill had invited me over, the way she'd prepared my favorite dish, the way she sat close to me, the way her knee kept touching mine, the excitement in her voice when she discussed my music—all this was telling me that I could have my way with her if I wanted. And I did want her. Yet I didn't. I didn't want to get involved with a woman, any woman, especially a woman I'd just met. And especially a woman who came on strong, the way Marla had come on strong. And especially a woman two years older than me and probably a lot more experienced.

"Mind if I read you a poem I wrote?" she asked.

I wanted to say no, but I didn't want to be rude. After all, she'd just cooked my dinner. She couldn't have been nicer.

"Sure," I said.

"I call it 'Lonely'—

"Lonely comes 'round like an uninvited guest
At the end of every day
Lonely sits right down on my bed
And promises not to stay
Lonely says he's just passing through

He won't bother me for long
But when morning comes I can still hear
Lonely singing this lonely song."

Without thinking, I reached for Jill's guitar and started singing what I heard as the chorus to the song. I don't know where the words came from. They just flowed.

Lonely in my heart, lonely in my soul
Lonely in summer's warmth
Lonely in winter's cold
Lonely until I can find
Someone to love me true
Lonely as I wonder,
Could that someone be you?

Jill looked at me in wonderment. "How did you do that?" she asked. "How did you know that was just what I wanted to say?"

"I'm . . . I'm really not sure . . . the words just kinda spilled out . . ."

She leaned over and gently took the guitar from my arms, pressed herself against me and put her mouth on mine. Her lips were moist. I could feel the swell of her breast and the throb of her beating heart.

"I'm sorry," I said. "I really am. But I've got to go."

Before she could protest, I was up and gone.

I'm writing on gray paper 'cause gun-metal gray is the color of war. There was a war inside my head. If I could find paper the color of camouflage, I'd use it to show how I tried to hide from the warfare. But there was no hiding. The battle was on.

One side said stay away from Jill. Jill was trouble. Jill was like Marla. She was eager—way too eager—to get with me. Maybe she wasn't as aggressive as Marla, but she sure as hell made it plain that she was mine for the asking. And also like Marla, she claimed to be connected to my music. Okay, maybe Marla hadn't written poems the way Jill wrote poems. And sure, that "Lonely" poem touched my heart, and yes, I wrote the chorus in a way that felt . . . well, magical . . . but maybe it was black magic. Maybe women like Marla and Jill had a way of putting a spell on me. Maybe that's how they used me. And then abused me. And then left me high and dry.

But on the other side, Jill was beautiful, Jill was sexy, Jill had Vicky and Vicky was precious. Spending time with Vicky and Jill was the most fun I'd had in months. They were warm and welcoming and made me feel wanted. They were almost too good to be true. I wanted to trust that good feeling, but could I? Was I just being set up for another big fall?

The mental warfare was making me a little crazy. And when I went back to work the next day at the Ford dealership, I had a hard time concentrating on the few customers who wandered in to look at used cars. I half expected Jill to come over to the lot and say something to me, but she didn't. Well, why should she? Wasn't I the one who owed her an apology? Yet I didn't know what to say. So I avoided her.

That evening, when I got back to the apartment above the antiques store, I saw that Meg Newberry had slipped a note under the door. The note shocked me. It said Marla had been trying to reach me and left a number where I could call her. How did Marla know where to reach me? And what did she want? I wasn't sure I cared. Besides, I didn't have a phone. I didn't want to talk her anyway. That night I barely slept.

Next morning, I went to work. I was sitting in the little trailer office that looked over the used car lot. No customers in sight. The phone rang.

"Vernon, it's Jill." Her voice wasn't angry but it

also wasn't sweet. She sounded matter-of-fact when she said, "Marla is calling you. She's on line two."

"Oh" was all I could manage.

"Do you want to talk to her?" asked Jill.

"I don't know. I guess I should."

I stared at the blinking red button for a few seconds before I finally pressed it.

"Hi," I said. "How'd you know I was here?"

"It's a small town."

"Where are you?"

"Nashville."

"Why are you calling?" I asked.

"I'm flying to Reno to get our divorce. There'll be papers for you to sign. Where should I send them?"

"Doesn't matter," I said.

"It does matter. I want this thing over."

I gave her the address of the Newberrys' antiques shop.

"That's all I want," she said. And with that, she hung up. I held the phone to my ear. The dial tone seemed like the ugliest sound I'd ever heard.

The next thing I knew, I was walking over to the main building. I went into Ryan's office and told him, "I'm sorry, man, I really am. But this job isn't right for me. I'm no salesman. I'm sure you'll find someone a lot better than me."

"I understand," he said. "Maybe you just weren't cut out for normal work. Maybe you should just stick with your music."

"Maybe. Anyway, thanks, Ryan, for trying to help me out. See you around."

On the way to my car, I heard someone calling my name. It was Jill running after me.

"Where you going?" she asked. "What happened?"

"I quit."

"I figured you were going to quit. I mean what happened on the phone with Marla?"

"Do you really care?"

"Yes, I really care."

"She said she'd be sending me divorce papers."

"And that surprises you?"

"That just makes me feel like I need to be alone."

"Sorry for butting in."

Before I could say that I was sorry for hurting her feelings, Jill turned around and walked away.

After that, the mental warfare got worse. I hated myself for getting down about the divorce. Shouldn't I be glad? Why did I have to see it as such a failure? Well, because it *was* a failure. I had failed at the only real relationship I'd ever had with a woman. I'd misread her completely. I'd been blind, stupid, deaf and dumb.

Holed up in the apartment above the antiques store, I withdrew for days. I kept the lights off, the shades drawn, the door locked. I stayed in bed, covering myself in darkness. I tried busting through the darkness by picking up the guitar and playing Skeeter's song—*Easygoing when it's good, easygoing when it's bad, easygoing when you happy, easygoing when you sad*—but it wasn't easy. It was hard. The long nights were endless. The days dragged on.

Concerned about my welfare, Meg and Tom offered me a job in their store. But if I couldn't sell used cars, I sure as hell couldn't sell used furniture. I thanked them but declined. Meg brought me a couple of meals, but I had no appetite. Tom asked me whether I'd ever thought about working in the oil fields in West Texas. I said I hadn't. I said not to worry. I'd be fine. I'd figure out something to do. But I didn't. I stayed down. I was lost.

White paper 'cause light broke through.

A week into this darkness, I heard a knock on my door. It was a Saturday night. It was Jill. She looked different. She had pulled her hair back into a ponytail. She looked great.

"Do you know what I think?" she asked before I could ask her in.

"No."

"I think you're feeling sorry for yourself. I think you're drowning in an ocean of self-pity—that's what I think."

I then said something that surprised me. I said, "I'm glad to see you, Jill."

"You are? I didn't think you ever wanted to see me again."

"I'm sorry if I gave you that feeling."

"You ran from my house."

"I was scared."

"Of what?" she asked.

"Of you," I said.

"So why are you glad to see me?"

"I don't feel scared anymore."

"Does that mean you're gonna invite me in?"

"Sure. Come in. I wish I had something to offer you."

"I don't need anything. Well, actually I do. I need you to listen to me."

"I'll try."

Jill came in and sat on a folding chair. I sat across from her on a broken-down couch.

"Where's Vicky?" I asked.

"Funny you ask 'cause she keeps asking, 'Where's Vernon?' Vicky's with my mom. Look, Vernon, Vicky saw something in you. I saw something in you. The thing we both saw is real. It's called goodness. You're a good guy, and you're a talented guy, and you need to do better than beat yourself up for choosing the wrong woman. Choosing the wrong mate is the most common mistake in the history of the world. I made that mistake. My sister Cynthia made that mistake. Who hasn't made that mistake?"

"'Cause everyone does it, doesn't make it easier."

"But it makes it more understandable. You can do something foolish without branding yourself a fool for the rest of your life. Which brings me to my main point—the rest of your life. What are you going do with it?"

"I don't know."

"Well, I do. You're gonna get outta here and sing, and write, and bring people pleasure by performing in front of them."

"I am?"

"Yes, you are."

At this point, in spite of myself, I found myself smiling. I couldn't resist Jill's attitude.

"See that," she said, "you're feeling better already. And you're gonna feel even better when I tell you about a friend of mine in Austin. He just bought a bar on Guadalupe Street, just down the street from the university. He wasn't gonna have live music, but I've convinced him he needs it."

"How do you know this guy?"

"He's an old boyfriend."

My heart sank. I saw her old boyfriend becoming her new boyfriend.

"I don't need to get mixed up with your boyfriends," I said.

"Former boyfriend. Very former. Now he's very married. Good guy. He told me to bring you down so he can hear you play tonight."

"Tonight? I don't have a band."

"He doesn't want a band. He doesn't have room for a band. Just you and your guitar."

"I've never done that before."

"You did it last week in front of me and Vicky."

"That was different."

"You'll do fine. Let's go."

"What songs am I gonna play?"

“You have dozens.”

“Dozens written for the band—and for Marla or Willard to sing.”

“Do you know the lyrics?”

“Sure, I wrote them.”

“Then you’ll do great. Hurry.”

“I need to change,” I said.

“Why?”

“I’m wearing jeans and an old work shirt.”

“The perfect uniform for a college bar,” said Jill. “Grab your guitar. Let’s go.”

We took the twenty-five-minute drive to Austin in Jill’s Country Squire Ford station wagon.

“Why the big car?” I asked.

“Ryan let me have it for practically nothing. It’s a good car for the long road trips Vicky and I like to take.”

As Jill described some of those trips, I zoned out. My head was filled with nervousness. Thinking of the songs I wanted to play, I couldn’t remember the lyrics. I wasn’t even sure I knew the melodies. I didn’t see myself as an artist who could sit on a stool and sing songs for an hour. I was just the guitarist, the guy in the background. I had no business being out front. This was all wrong.

“You’re awfully quiet,” said Jill as we entered the Austin city limits.

“I’m worried,” I confessed.

“I’m not.”

When we pulled up to the club, my stomach was in knots. For a second, I thought of bolting. Then I looked up and saw the big bright blue neon sign in the window: SKEETER’S.

I couldn’t believe it. Could it be the same Skeeter that I’d known?

“Vernon,” said Jill as we walked through the front door, “meet Bobby Marks. This is his bar.”

“Why’d you call it ‘Skeeter’s’?” was the first thing I asked.

“For an old guitarist and family friend. He died last week,” said Bobby. “He was the first guy to introduce me to music. He was a famous instrument repairman here in Austin. Could have been a famous guitarist, too, but he was afraid of playing in front of crowds.”

“He was my teacher,” I said, stunned by his connection to Bobby.

“Well, that’s beautiful,” said Jill. “Proof that positive forces are bringing us all together tonight.”

“If Skeeter was your teacher,” said Bobby, “I know

he must have taught you the blues. Maybe you want to start off tonight with some blues."

What a great suggestion! What a great feeling to know that Skeeter's spirit was with me!

Jam-packed with college kids, the place was bigger than I'd expected. There were actually two bars, one along the back wall and one on the side. Practically everyone was drinking Lone Star or Pearl beer. Lots of loud talk, lots of young guys and pretty girls. You could feel the sexual energy. I wasn't sure how a solo singer would go over, but looking over at that SKEETER'S sign in the window, I realized my own energy was pretty high.

There was no bandstand. A stool was placed in a corner next to the back bar. I plugged in my amp. I was given a mic. There was no spotlight, which was fine with me. There was no introduction, also fine with me. I took Bobby's suggestion and broke out with a blues, one of the first blues Skeeter had ever taught me—Elmore James's "Dust My Broom." That got the attention of a few guys who wandered over to see who was playing. I stayed on the blues 'cause the blues were warming me up. At first, my singing voice sounded a little unsure, but when I heard Jill shout, "Sing out, boy! Say what you got to say!" I broke out in a big smile. My voice got louder. I actually liked the sound of my voice. Singing these old blues brought Skeeter to mind. I pictured him out there, standing among the college kids, nodding his head and cheering me on. I hit notes I'd never hit before, sang songs I'd never sung before, felt feelings I'd never felt before. The small circle surrounding me grew larger. The cheers after each song got louder. When I broke into Jimmy Reed's "Bright Lights Big City," some of the kids started dancing. The only percussion was my foot stomping the floor. No one seemed to care. The music was getting over.

After a half hour or so, I turned to my music, songs like "Faith" and "Dreamin' in Blue" and "Cheatin' Days." By then I had the crowd in the palm of my hand. When I sang my slow songs, the place got whisper quiet. When I sang the rockers, everyone got to dancing. When I'd sung for well over an hour, Bobby came over and whispered in my ear, "Keep going if you like. The tip jar's overflowing."

By the time the place closed down, I'd sung three sets and cleared two hundred dollars. Bobby wanted me back for next Friday and Saturday.

"Okay, Mr. Crabbypants," said Jill, "what you got to complain about now?"

"Nothing," I said. "Nothing at all."

On the way back to Round Rock, the highway was

covered in moonlight. I felt like the moonlight was meant just for me—and Jill. When we got to the antiques store, she parked the car. We stayed silent for a long while.

"Well?" she asked.

"I'm not tired," I said. "I'm still bouncing off the music."

"Me too."

"Wanna come up?" I asked.

"Thought you'd never ask," she answered.

"What about Vicky?"

"Mom's staying over."

"Your mom doesn't mind you being out all night?"

"Mom's used to my wild ways. She tried to turn me into a sorority girl like my sister Cynthia, but soon saw it wasn't gonna work. She gave up trying to reform me long ago."

We got out of the car. I followed her up the narrow staircase to my tiny apartment. I'm not sure what I was feeling—happy for the great gig at Skeeter's, grateful that Jill had coaxed me into it, uneasy about what we were going to do. I'd never been with any woman other than Marla. In bed, Marla had lots of quirks and demands. I couldn't help but wonder whether Jill was the same. My wondering didn't last long.

Jill's only concern was pleasing me.

"You've had it rough," she said. "But I'm here to show you not all women are users. Some actually like men—and like supporting them."

My mind said, *I could use all the support I can get*—but my mouth didn't speak the words. I didn't have to speak. Jill sensed how I felt. She knew that my soul was wounded and my body was hungry for love. She provided that love in ways that were beautiful. When morning broke and sunlight flooded my little bedroom, the hunger had lifted. Finally, I was a man at peace with the world.

After that, everything fell into place. There was a natural rhythm to my new life with Jill and Vicky. I went over there every night for dinner. It felt like family. After a few weeks, I began spending the night there. That made Jill even happier, not to mention me. Thanking Meg and Tom Newberry for their kindness, I moved out of the apartment and in with Jill, Vicky and Toby. Skeeter's turned into a five-night-a-week gig, meaning I was making decent money.

In her own determined way, Jill kept encouraging and pushing me. She got someone at the Austin newspaper to write about me. The reporter actually owned the two Good Friends albums and said he'd been wondering what had happened to the guitarist. His article was flattering. That led to work at a folk club in Houston close to Rice University. No band, just me. By this time, I was comfortable up there on the stool, just singing my songs.

"You know what," Jill said one Saturday morning, "I think I could manage you."

"What do you think you've been doing?"

"I mean for real. Not part-time. I think if I put all my efforts into your musical career, you could really get somewhere. And I don't mean because of my efforts, I mean because of your talents. All you need is a steady push."

I had no arguments. Playing clubs as a stand-alone artist gave me a freedom I'd never felt before. There were no band members to contend with, no personal conflicts, no brutal ego battles. It was a pleasure to be able to think about nothing except my singing, my songs and my playing.

After Houston, Jill found a coffeehouse on McKinney Avenue in Dallas where a poet had been holding court. The owner was open to giving me a tryout. Jill, Vicky, Toby and I spent the weekend in a motel up there. The owner liked my stuff and booked me for a couple of weeks. Dallas led to a gig in Fort Worth out by Texas Christian University. Seeing that my biggest fans were college kids, Jill concentrated on that circuit. She worked like a demon.

"You know what," she said, in her always upbeat manner, "I think we should relocate."

"Why do you say that?"

"I think we should be operating out of a more centrally located city. Move into the big time. Better contacts. More connections."

"What about your job?"

"I'm ready to give it up. It's not nearly as much fun as managing you. Besides, I can find work as a bookkeeper anywhere."

"That's a risky move," I said.

"No risk, no reward. Besides, much as we love Round Rock, we all need a breath of fresh air. New city, new possibilities."

"Where are you thinking?"

"Maybe Dallas."

"Living in Dallas would be a whole lot more expensive than living here."

"Or Fort Worth. Fort Worth's cheaper."

"I like Fort Worth. How do you think Vicky would feel about it?" I asked. "We'd have to pull her out of school."

"Every day that Vicky wakes up and sees you and

me together, she's the happiest girl in Texas. Vicky's an adaptable kid."

"Well, if we're going to do this, I suppose we oughta get married."

"What!" Jill screamed. "Why in hell would we go and do something stupid like that?"

"We're living together. We're already a family. Might as well make it official."

"You've already tried that and it turned to shit. What's the point of trying it again?"

"All I'm saying is that we could make it legal."

"There's nothing illegal about our love, Vernon. To me it's more than legal. It's the most beautiful thing I've ever felt."

"You know I feel the same."

"Then we're good. Like the old folks say, 'If the damn thing ain't broke, don't try and fix it.'"

Green paper for a green light that said, "Get moving." The move didn't take long. When Jill makes up her mind to do something, it gets done in a hurry. We were out of Round Rock in less than a month.

It was an especially good month because Jill found herself writing poems like crazy. A lot of them were about me and our love. When she showed them to me,

I immediately heard melodies. Each word seemed to carry a musical note. She called one poem, my favorite, "Surprising Love":

Thought the dark would last forever
And night would never end
I couldn't see past sadness
Couldn't see beyond the bend
But then you appeared from out of the blue
Like a blessing from above
You showed up and brought with you
A beautiful surprising love
A surprising love
That changed my life in every way
A surprising love
I've come to cherish every day

I put the words to music, and "Surprising Love," along with a half-dozen other songs Jill and I wrote together, became part of my repertoire.

"We're so good together," she said to me. "We're good together in every possible way."

"You'll get no arguments from me."

"I don't want any arguments. I've had enough arguments with old boyfriends to last a lifetime. I just want harmony. I don't want the music to ever stop."

“It won’t,” I assured her.

It didn’t. It kept getting better. Every day in every way, life was great. We rented a small house on the west side of Fort Worth with a fenced-in backyard big enough for a swing set for Vicky and a doghouse for Toby. The elementary school was right around the corner.

Jill was forever on the phone finding places for me to play weekends. She booked me at coffeehouses close to the big state universities in Norman, Oklahoma; Fayetteville, Arkansas; and Shreveport, Louisiana. We went together everywhere as a family. Sometimes Jill would take Vicky to the gigs. If you can believe it, that little girl had learned the lyrics to all my songs and, giving me the biggest smile in the world, would mouth my words as she silently sang along with me.

I was hardly making a fortune, but enough to get by. Jill, who was great at managing everything—especially money—had found part-time work keeping the books for a dress shop in downtown Fort Worth. We settled in a sweet routine that had me picking up Vicky from school during the week while, on weekends, we all headed out to wherever I was working.

Come Christmastime I’d been gigging on this circuit a couple of months.

“Let’s spend the holidays in Nashville,” said Jill.

“What’s in Nashville?”

“A club where all the record execs go to discover new talent. Turns out the owner heard about you from someone who saw you in Shreveport. Now he wants to see you for himself. Meanwhile, I’ve been talking to some execs at RCA and Capitol. I think I got them interested.”

“In a solo singer without a band?”

“You can always put a band together, Vernon. Nashville’s overrun with good musicians.”

“Everything’s going so good here in Fort Worth.”

“Fort Worth is a stepping-stone. We can’t stop here. We gotta go on. One of those A and R guys even knew about Good Friends. He’s originally from Austin and remembered when ‘Faith’ was on the radio. He’s ready to give you a fair hearing.”

“I’m not sure.”

“I am. I told him about all this great new material we got. I told him how the college kids go crazy for your stuff. What do you say?”

“You got your job.”

“They’re letting me off the week between Christmas and New Year’s. No problem.”

“I guess it makes sense.”

"Perfect sense."

With that, Jill hugged me tight and hurried to the kitchen to start dinner.

No more pretty paper. If I could write on black paper, I would. Dark gray will have to do.

We left the day after spending Christmas with Jill's whole family. The night before, I had a nightmare. I can't remember what I dreamt, but it was so terrible I woke up in a sweat and must have screamed because I startled Jill. She kissed me gently on the forehead, put her arms around me and told me to go back to sleep. I slept uneasily and awoke at dawn, feeling shaky and unsettled.

We packed up the station wagon and headed out early. I was driving, Jill next to me and Vicky in the backseat with Toby on her lap. At first we were to leave the dog with Jill's mom, but Vicky threw a fit, so we figured we'd just have to find a motel that allowed pets. We stopped in Texarkana for a late lunch at a barbecue joint. I can still see Toby going to town on those rib bones. Must have been three or four p.m. when we headed into the low-rise mountains outside Hot Springs, Arkansas. That's when the rains began.

A drizzle quickly turned into a steady downpour. Then the downpour turned into a deluge.

Sensing I was a little nervous, Jill said, "I love the rain. Love to watch the rain against the windshield. Love how it makes us feel so cozy inside. Let's sing the rain song, Vicky. What do you say?"

Together, they sang:

"Rain rain go away
Come back another day
Little Vicky wants to play
So please make everything okay."

The last thing I remember is the sound of them singing. I still hear that sound every night when I go to sleep.

"Rain rain go away
Come back another day
Little Vicky wants to play
So please make everything okay."

I blocked it out. I blocked out all the events that were explained to me when, days later, I woke up in a Hot Springs hospital. I blocked out the sight of an eighteen-wheeler barreling around the mountain bend. I blocked out the explosion of the truck crashing head-on into us. I blocked out the station wagon flipping over on its side. I blocked out being thrown from the car. I blocked out the truck driver, who wasn't hurt, yelling at me not to crawl under the station wagon where I was trying to get to Jill and Vicky. I blocked out the station wagon collapsing on my legs.

My legs.

I could feel them but I couldn't see them. I reached down to touch them. Was it all just a bad dream?

"We had no choice," the doctor said.

A lightning bolt of terror struck my heart. "Where's Jill? Where's Vicky? Where's Toby?" I asked.

"It was sudden. They experienced no pain."

No pain—I thought to myself.

No pain.

They experienced no pain.

"Rain rain go away
Come back another day
Little Vicky wants to play
So please make everything okay."

NO MORE PRETTY PAPER

It's hard for me to cry. Maybe it's just a man thing. Maybe it's 'cause I'm used to sitting on my emotions. Whatever the reasons, I can count the times I've actually wept.

This was one of those times. I put down the last sheet of gray paper with Vernon's story and felt hot tears streaming down my cheeks. The rain song that Vernon heard little Vicky sing was ringing in my ears.

Sitting in that worn-out easy chair in the Western Hotel, I felt drained. I felt frustrated that I had no more papers, frustrated that I didn't know where Vernon was, and even if I did know, I wouldn't know what to do. I wouldn't know how to help him. Feeling foolish and hopeless, I wiped away the tears. I stood up and went to the window. It was a dark, gloomy October night. The neon of the Leonards department store sign lit the spot where I had first seen Vernon. I stared at that spot for a long time.

Now I knew why when he cried "pretty paper" there was so much pain in his voice. Now I knew what he'd gone through, what he had gained and what he had lost.

I went back to the easy chair, sat down and looked at the pile of paper I'd just read. I sighed a big sigh. All I could do was go to sleep, get up the next morning and, together with Brother Paul and the rest of the band, hit the road. It chilled me to remember that our next gig, my last for a while, was in Little Rock, where, on the way, we'd be driving through Hot Springs.

I don't know what to make of the fact that our van broke down in Hot Springs. Piston and spark plug problems. We had to be hauled into a repair shop. They said it'd take a couple of hours to get us back on the road and pointed us to a café four blocks away. Walking those blocks with Brother Paul and the boys in the band, I looked up and saw that the café sat directly across the street from St. Joseph's Hospital. I imagined that's where Vernon had been brought after the crash.

All this meant, of course, that I couldn't stop thinking about Vernon even if I wanted to. I wondered if, once again, there was some cosmic conspiracy at work to keep Vernon right in front of me. And if there was, what did the cosmos want me to do? I thought back to my Sunday school class and remembered what I had told the kids when they asked me what good deeds I was doing. "I'm working on a good cause," I had said, "and you all have inspired me to keep at it."

Well, what exactly was I keeping at? Reading Vernon's story inspired me more than ever to help the guy, but how can you help a guy who's disappeared without a trace? And besides, I still didn't know what kind of help he needed. I was stuck.

"You talk to Crash?" asked Brother Paul after downing a cheeseburger and a big slice of apple pie.

Crash Stewart was the promoter booking our gigs.

"Not for a while."

"He called you in Fort Worth when you were out. I slipped the message under your door."

"Didn't see it."

"Maybe he's got something up his sleeve," said Paul.

"He usually does."

The apple pie looked good, and I ordered a piece for

myself. I drank a cup of coffee, got a couple of bucks' worth of change and headed to the pay phone on the back wall of the café.

Soon as Crash picked up, I asked, "What you got cooking?"

"The Longhorn Ballroom in Dallas."

"When?"

"Thanksgiving holiday. Four nights. Thursday through Sunday."

"That's a long ways off."

"Ain't that long."

"How do I get by from now till Thanksgiving?"

"Go back to Nashville. Write songs."

"I'm fresh out of ideas."

"You'll get an idea. You always do."

"This time I'm really dry," I said.

"Have a drink."

"Drinking doesn't help."

"Helps me."

"But you're not writing. You're promoting."

"Promotin' ain't all that different from writin'. It's creative as all hell."

"Well, if you create some more work for me, lemme know."

"Will do."

The news of work, even though it was a ways off,

helped my disposition. The car got fixed in time for us to make the Little Rock gig. Next morning we drove to Nashville, where I got reacquainted with the wife and kids and did manage to write a batch of new songs.

More good news came in the form of a hefty royalty check from my song "Pretty Paper" that Roy Orbison had sung and released. The tune was a hit. Of course cashing that check was another reason I couldn't get Vernon off my mind. It'd been ten months since I'd first spotted him in front of Leonards—and not a day had passed in those ten months without me wondering about his fate.

One morning in late October, I was driving out to my publisher's office in Goodlettsville, some twenty miles outside Nashville, where I was paid to sit and write songs. I had the radio on one of the country stations when the deejay said how happy he was to have Bambi Love in the studio with him to talk about her new release.

"It's called 'Crazy Love Is Good Love,'" she said. "Proud to say it's something I wrote myself. Well, truth is, I cowrote it with my fiancé."

"You're talking about your producer, Slick Walters."

"I don't really write music. That's Slick's department. But I wrote the story. I've always been a storyteller. Slick says I'm a natural."

"Speaking of stories," said the deejay, "tell me something of your story. Where'd you grow up? What's your background?"

"I'm a country girl from Wyoming. Daddy was a cowboy who worked the rodeo circuit. He roped the calves and rode the bulls. Mama was a beauty queen. She wanted me to follow in her footsteps and put me in pageants from third grade on. She's the one who pushed me into show business."

"How'd the music thing start?"

"Slick heard me singing the national anthem at one of Daddy's rodeos in Arizona. He said I had the best voice he'd heard since Brenda Lee. He said he'd make me a star."

I couldn't believe it. She was making the whole thing up.

"Looks like he's making good on that promise."

"He sure is," she said.

"I know Slick has his studio right here in Nashville. I'm guessing you've made Nashville your home."

"It was for a while, but right now I'm just passing

through to introduce my new single. Slick knows I don't love the cold, so he found us a place in Miami for the winter."

"Tennessee's loss is Florida's gain. Thanks for dropping by, Bambi, and best of luck with the new single. Let's give it a listen right now. Here's Miss Bambi Love doing 'Crazy Love Is Good Love.'"

It was an up-tempo catchy kind of tune with lyrics that didn't make a whole lot of sense—as if that mattered. Lots of hit songs don't make sense. And if I had to guess, this song, a dance number, was gonna be a hit. The minute it was over, I turned off the radio.

Talk about a devil woman, I thought to myself. Hell, this gal gave poison widows a good name.

Couldn't write any songs that day 'cause my head was filled with "Crazy Love Is Good Love." When I got home that night, I listened to that second Good Friends album and discovered the same rhythm and melody in Vernon's song called "Wild Country Night." All Bambi and Slick had done was slap on some silly new lyrics.

I got good and mad. I cussed out Slick and I cussed out this hussy Bambi. There wasn't anyone around to hear—the house was empty—so all this cussing felt a little foolish. But I did it anyway. I slammed my hand down on the table. I went out to the garage, where I kept a punching bag, and I pounded the thing till my knuckles hurt.

I wanted to do something.

I had to do something.

This was wrong.

This needed to be made right.

I was tired of the all the signs coming my way, giving me clues of what happened. I was tired of reading about the story, tired of thinking about the story. I didn't know whether I'd been flirting with this story or whether this story had been flirting with me. Either way, I was outside the story looking in. I wanted to be inside the story. If I really cared about this guy and the god-awful bad breaks he'd gotten—and was still getting—it was sure as hell time to finally get hold of this story and bend it my way.

It was time to get going.

ROUND ROCK, TEXAS

Round Rock is an easy town to overlook. Driving down I-35 from Dallas, you zip through Waco, Temple, Belton and Georgetown. If you blink, you miss Round Rock before sailing into Austin.

I was in a hurry to get there. I'd started the trip in Dallas, where Crash had booked me into Dewey Groom's Longhorn Ballroom over the Thanksgiving weekend. I'd been making calls to Round Rock long before that, though, with no results.

The first call was to the Smith Ford dealership, but the operator said it no longer existed. When I contacted Lone Star Ford of Round Rock, I was told that the Smiths had sold out years ago. Information had no number for Ryan Smith. I remembered that Cynthia's maiden name was Simone and her mom's first name was Virginia. There were only two Simones in Round Rock—Fred and Reggie. When I got Fred on the phone, he spoke with a shaky voice. He sounded very old. Turned out he was a distant relative of Reggie, who he said was married to Virginia. At last I was getting somewhere. At last I was about to talk to people—the parents of Cynthia and Jill—who had a direct link to Vernon. But no one answered at that number. I called at least ten times. I let the phone ring and ring, but it was no use.

That's when I decided that, the minute the Dallas gig was over Sunday night, I'd jump in my car Monday morning, head due south and see if I could get to the bottom of this thing.

Arriving in Round Rock, I rode around until I spotted Luby's cafeteria, remembering it as the place where Vernon's grandmother had worked. It was lunchtime. I had chicken-fried steak, mashed potatoes, a nice chunk of cornbread and sweet iced tea. I gave myself a few minutes to digest before heading to the pay phone behind the cashier. A phone book was attached to the wall by a chain. I looked up Reggie Simone's number and, figuring what the hell, gave it

one more try. No answer. I wrote down the address. The cashier knew the street and gave me directions.

The Simone residence was a handsome ranch-style house, the nicest in the neighborhood. I pressed the doorbell and heard chimes ring out. Waited a few minutes and rang the chimes again. No one came. I walked around to the two-car garage but the windowless garage door was closed tight.

All I could do was return to my car and call it a day. That's when a woman, taking her brown-and-white cocker spaniel for a walk, asked, "Looking for Reggie and Virginia?"

"I am."

"They've been spending most of their time in Dallas."

"I was actually looking for Virginia's daughter, Cynthia, and her husband, Ryan."

"They moved to Dallas. That's the reason Reggie and Virginia are there. Just a week or so ago, Cynthia had a baby girl."

"I see. Well, thank you, ma'am. One other thing—you wouldn't happen to have a number for them in Dallas, would you?"

"Virginia gave me Cynthia's number, in case of an emergency. Is this an emergency?"

"I'd say it is."

"Wait here. I live right next door. I'll get the number for you."

The number in hand, I pulled into the first gas station I came across. I got out and headed for the pay phone. The long-distance operator connected me to Dallas.

"Could I be talking to Cynthia Smith?" I asked.

"You could be. Who is this?"

I introduced myself. "I'm a friend of Vernon Clay's."

"You are?"

"I most surely am."

"Well then, you'll be wanting to talk to him. He's

here. But it'll take a little while for him to get to the phone. Can you wait?"

"I can."

My heart was racing. After all this time, I'd actually located my man.

"Who's this?" The question came from a man with a deeply skeptical voice.

I told him before adding, "Been wondering where in hell you been keeping yourself."

A few seconds passed before he said, "I figured that if you wanted to find me, you would."

"You haven't made it easy."

"I never really know where I'm going till I get there."

"You gonna stay still in Dallas long enough for me to drive back up there and see you?" I asked.

"For what reason?"

"Well, you sent me your story—that's reason enough. I got some ideas for the next chapter."

More long seconds of silence.

"Where are you now?" he asked.

"Fresh from a delicious chicken-fried steak lunch at Luby's cafeteria in Round Rock."

I thought I heard him chuckle.

"Hell," he finally said, "if you're that gung ho to see me, Cynthia will give you the address."

I felt a little foolish turning around and retracing my route a hundred and eighty miles back to Dallas, where I'd started out earlier that same day. Felt like I was running around in circles. In fact, I'd been doing just that. On the bright side, though, I'd accomplished something. I had my target in sight.

I got to Dallas too late in the night to pay a visit, but by noon the next day, I was knocking on the door of a two-story Colonial-style brick home on Beverly Drive in Highland Park, the fanciest section of the city.

A well-coiffed woman in her mid-fifties answered the door. She was dressed in a tailored gray dress adorned by a string of cultured pearls. She was attractive in a matronly way, poised and reserved.

"Yes?" she asked sternly.

Introducing myself, I said, "I believe Cynthia and Vernon are expecting me."

"Oh, you're the *musician* friend," she said, stressing the word "musician" as if it were akin to being a criminal.

Just then a younger woman appeared, holding a sleeping infant. I recognized Cynthia from her Good Friends photos. She was a striking brunette with soft brown eyes and a graceful bearing. She wore a housecoat elaborately embroidered with figures of swans.

"Forgive my appearance," she said. "I was just nursing."

"This must be the new addition," I said. "Congratulations. She's a beauty."

"Thank you. Would you mind coming into the den so we could chat for a while?"

"Sure thing."

Without uttering a word, the disapproving mother disappeared up the stairs.

The spacious den had floor-to-ceiling windows overlooking a lush garden and an oval-shaped pool. Cynthia sat on a pale blue couch. I sat across from her in a large leather armchair. Nestled in Cynthia's arms, the infant continued her peaceful sleep.

"You'll have to forgive my mother," said Cynthia. "She bristles at anything or anyone that reminds her of my former life. She hates that Vernon's living with us—so much so that I was shocked when she and Dad came to help out with the baby."

"How long has Vernon been living here?"

"Not too long after Ryan sold the dealership in Round Rock and opened one here in Dallas. Must have been around Easter when I went over to Fort

Worth and happened to see him selling his wrapping papers and ribbons. After the accident, we had no idea where he went. He just disappeared into thin air. You can imagine my shock when I saw him there on the sidewalk. At first I couldn't believe it. But it was really him. I knew I had to do something. Before I even approached Vernon, I went home and spoke to Ryan. Ryan has a heart of gold. He agreed with me. We had to do something. So I went back to Fort Worth. Vernon wasn't all that glad to see me. I understood. I'm sure that seeing me only made him see Jill and Vicky. At first he wouldn't even talk to me, but I was persistent. I found out where he was living. I'm sure the people who owned that little restaurant treated him kindly, but hawking his wares in all kinds of weather in front of that department store, day after day—it had to be hard on him. It took a while, but I finally convinced him to try an easier life."

"And has it been easier?" I asked.

"Not really. He's not happy. He rarely comes out of his room. And now that my parents are here, he won't come out at all."

"What does he do in there?"

"For a while I saw that he was writing."

"I know. I read what he'd written. He sent it to the

good folks who owned the restaurant, and they gave it to me."

"And then he stopped writing. I'm guessing he wrote out his story. But why did he send it to you?"

"I'm not exactly sure," I said. "But I'd like to believe he's reaching out for help."

"So you're here to help him. How?"

"Wish I could say. Like you, I first saw him out there by Leonards. Ever since then, his story has been following me wherever I go."

"I suppose you know how Marla dropped Willard for some Nashville producer. Willard joined the navy. Now Marla's calling herself Bambi Love. That woman makes me sick."

"Does Vernon know about Bambi?" I asked.

"When I mentioned it, he cut me off. He didn't want to hear another word."

"Well, I admire you and your husband for putting yourself out for him."

"We haven't done all that much. In practical terms, I know he's better off. But emotionally, I'm not sure."

The baby began to cry.

"What's her name?" I asked.

"Jill."

"Does it comfort Vernon to be around her?"

"He can't look at her without crying," said Cynthia. "So he mainly stays away."

"I best go back there and tell him hello, if that's okay with you."

"I'm glad you came. I really am. I just hope he'll talk to you."

"We'll see."

Outside, the November sun was bright, but the air was cold. I knocked on the pool house door. A few seconds went by before I heard the sound of rolling wheels. The door opened and I looked down at the man, still on the cart, who looked considerably older than when I had first seen him nearly a year before. His face was lined and his eyes were sad. Yet he hadn't lost his looks. His ruggedly handsome square-jawed face still retained vitality. Being in his presence, I felt a distinct strength radiating from him. He wore a white flannel shirt, snug enough to show the bulge of his biceps and shape of his broad shoulders. In the corner of the surprisingly large room, I noticed a set of exercise equipment.

"Looks like you've been working out," I said.

"A way to pass the time."

"By the way, it's good to see you, man. It really is."

"And why is that?" he asked.

"You been on my mind. Thanks for sending me your story."

"You were curious," he said.

"And remain so."

"About what?"

"Like I said on the phone, I'm curious about the next chapter."

"This is it," he said, waving his arms around the room. "This is me. A bird in a gilded cage."

"But has the bird been singing?"

I was hoping that would get a laugh, but it didn't.

"Got nothing to sing about," he said.

"Hell, man, you got a shitload of songs."

"Songs that have already been sung."

"Agreed. Not only have they been sung, they've been ripped off and resung by your former singer. But you know all about that."

"I don't know much about anything."

"Well, sir," I said, "it's time you learned. You got a producer out there cannibalizing your catalogue. The bastard's flat-out stealing you blind."

"Good for him."

"Really?" I asked. "That's how you really feel about it? You really like the idea of some snake in the grass making a fortune on hit songs that were born out of your heart and soul?"

"You read my story," said Vernon. "You know it just don't have no happy endings. Things start out bad, then get better, then get worse. There ain't no changing that."

"I'm not sure."

"I am."

"So what's your plan?" I asked.

"To have no plans. To give up on plans. To stay where I am. To know this is as good as it's gonna get. I got food, I got shelter. I got a couple of good friends. I won't go out there and disturb the world as long as the world don't come in here and disturb me."

"But you gotta face facts, Vernon—the world *is* disturbing you. It's disturbing the hell outta you. You got every damn reason under the sun to be disturbed. Fact is, I've come here to disturb you even more."

He finally laughed, but more a laugh of scorn than amusement.

With determined eyes, he looked at me and said, "I hate that you had to come such a long way to find this out, but the truth is pretty simple. The truth is that at this point, I really can't be disturbed."

"You mean, that wall you built around you is so high no one's climbing over it?" I asked.

"Something like that."

"Well, I've climbed over it. I'm here, aren't I?"

"For a very short while."

I went over to one of those beanbag chairs that had been set up in front of a TV. I plopped down and surprised myself by saying, "Hey, man, I got all the time in the world."

NUTSY PERKINS AND RANGER ROY FINKELSTEIN

Brother Paul was a good drummer and an even better friend. The best thing about Paul was how he stayed in contact with all his many connections. For a tough guy, he had few enemies. Other tough guys respected him because he had balls of steel.

Paul and I were in Fort Worth, where he'd gone to see his mother. For old times' sake, he suggested we meet for a drink at Big Bill's barroom. The last thing I told Vernon when he was giving me the silent treatment in Dallas was that, whether he liked it or not, I'd come up with a plan. But of course I had no plan. Over a few beers and bourbon chasers, I explained my predicament to Brother Paul.

"You need help," said Paul.

"You ain't kidding."

"I think I know the guys. You know them too."

"I do?"

"Nutsy and Ranger Roy."

"Nutsy Perkins? Ranger Roy Finkelstein? How could they help?"

"They're idea men."

"They are?"

"Yes, sir. They're never out of ideas. I was just talking to them yesterday. They moved up to Denton."

"I heard about that. Why Denton?"

"Fort Worth was getting a little hot for them. Denton's off the beaten track. I'll tell 'em you wanna see 'em."

"I don't see the point."

"You and me, we don't see a lot of things," said Paul. "But Nutsy and Ranger Roy have their ways. I'll call them. I'll set up a meeting."

"Still don't know what good that'll do."

"It sure as shit won't do no harm."

Nutsy, who was no music fan, had reservations about the meeting. Ranger Roy, a big fan, had none.

The only caveat was that I'd have to go to Denton, headquarters of their growing enterprise.

I didn't mind the forty-minute drive. I had fond memories of Denton. Last time I played a honky-tonk in that vicinity, I happened by North Texas State University, where the school jazz band sounded as good as anything by Stan Kenton or Woody Herman. Funny to think of sleepy ol' Denton as a jazz town, but that's what it was.

Denton was also the perfect low-profile place for the kind of business Nutsy and Ranger Roy were engaged in. They operated out of a defunct funeral parlor situated next to an auto repair shop. They didn't bother to take down the sign that said PEACE VALLEY FUNERAL SERVICES AND CREMATION.

The door was open, so I walked right in. The place smelled of cigar smoke. The front room was empty.

"Anyone here?" I asked.

A gray-haired woman appeared and wanted to know my name. I told her.

"Wait here," she said.

She disappeared. Ten minutes went by before she returned to say, "Follow me."

She took me around back where we faced a good-sized warehouse with a front door of thick steel. She gave six short knocks that led to the door being unbolted.

"They're in that private office, way in the back," was all the woman said.

Inside the warehouse was a long row of desks piled up with papers. Stationed at the desk were men—some looked like bank clerks, some looked like farmhands—talking on the phone. Other men were racing back and forth, marking up several large blackboards where the results of sporting events were being posted. The place buzzed with excited chatter.

I spotted Nutsy and Ranger Roy in the private office closed off by glass. They sat at opposite ends of a big conference table covered with more piles of paper and six different phones. Nutsy, who was on a call, didn't acknowledge my presence, but Ranger Roy got right up to greet me.

"I see you found us," he said.

He wore a black cowboy hat with a silver sheriff's star stuck above the brim. His oversized frog eyes were friendly enough. He seemed genuinely glad to see me. He had all kinds of questions about the new songs I'd been writing. I asked him whether he'd given up the Record Dump in Garland.

"Hell, no," he said. "It's going stronger than ever. We got plans to open another store on Deep Ellum in

Dallas. I'm never giving up on the music business. Folks are always gonna need their music. It's just that the profit margins are slim. That's why I've had to move up here for a spell to help Nutsy smooth over our new setup."

"It's really something," I said as I looked around.

Nutsy concluded his phone call and finally looked over at me. He was wearing that same white fedora with a purple feather. His double-breasted suit was gray flannel with broad, chalky pinstripes.

"Last time I seen you," he said, "some dumb dame nearly cost you your life."

"I remember," I said.

"You still seeing her?" he asked.

I answered, "Only in my dreams."

Both men laughed.

"Tell me about your problem," said Roy. "Brother Paul says it's something about music."

"My partner's a music fanatic," Nutsy broke in. "He says there's big money in music. But I'll be damned if I ever figured out how to make any."

"Remember those albums you sold me by Good Friends?" I asked Ranger Roy.

"Sure thing," he said.

"Well, here's what happened after I took those records home and listened to them."

For the next fifteen minutes or so, I laid out the story of Vernon Clay, the hard times he'd endured and how he'd been screwed over. I'm not saying I'm the best storyteller in the world, but I'm not the worst. I realized that if there were ever a time to tell a story right—and make the right emotional impact—that time was now. I gave it my all.

When I was through, Ranger Roy had lots of questions about Vernon, Slick Walters and Bambi Love. I answered them as best I could. Roy was definitely interested, but Nutsy not so much.

"So what's in it for us?" Nutsy finally asked.

"To be honest," I said, "I really don't know. I'm only here 'cause Brother Paul thought you guys might have an idea."

"The idea of this here operation is to make money," said Nutsy. "What you got is a charity case. But we ain't no charity."

"I understand," I said. "Thanks for hearing me out."

Ranger Roy didn't say anything. For a second, he closed his eyes. When he opened them, I thought I saw a tear, but maybe I was imagining things.

"Any way you look at it," Roy said, "it's a helluva story. It's the kinda story that makes you think."

"That's the problem with you," said Nutsy. "You think too much."

How'd it go?" Brother Paul wanted to know as soon as I got back to Fort Worth.

"Your buddies are big-time bookies," I said. "They're out to make a buck."

"Aren't we all?"

"Suppose so."

"But what'd they say when you told 'em the story?"

"Not much."

"So they're thinking," said Paul.

"They're taking bets," I said.

"They put you in a poker game up there?"

"Ranger Roy mentioned something about it," I said, "but I wasn't in the mood."

"That's not like you," said Paul.

"I'm going over to Dallas to see Vernon. I got me an idea."

HIGH SOCIETY

I got the idea from a movie starring Bing Crosby, Frank Sinatra and Grace Kelly. It's a fluffy love story about rich folks in Newport, Rhode Island. The final scene, a fancy wedding, takes place in a mansion when, all of a sudden, Louis Armstrong and his All-Stars appear outside on the patio and start blowing their brand of hot jazz. The film's called *High Society*.

"I need a favor," I asked Cynthia when I called her the day after my Denton trip.

"What kind of favor?"

"Well, seems as though my promoter found me some bookings in the Dallas area. Looks like I'll be staying in Fort Worth through the holidays . . ."

"Your family back in Nashville can't be too happy about that."

"By now they're used to living with a traveling troubadour. If I can, I'm gonna bring 'em down here for New Year's. In the meantime, my band needs a place to rehearse. I got some new tunes to woodshed, and I was wondering if your pool house is available."

Silence on the other end.

"By any chance are these songs that Vernon could sing?" Cynthia asked with a smile in her voice.

"I suspect so. Or maybe he has his own songs he could teach us."

"You mention any of this to him?"

"I'm thinking this might be one of those times when action is better than words. What do you think will happen if I just show up with the band?"

"We'll just have to see, won't we?"

Me and the band arrived the next day around two in the afternoon. Cynthia led us out to the pool house, where Vernon was in the middle of his weight-lifting routine. Under his tank top, his muscular torso was covered in sweat.

"What the hell . . ." was the first thing he said when he saw me standing there with my Martin guitar. Behind me was Brother Paul hauling his drum gear, plus our bass player and lap steel guitarist.

"No worries, Vernon," I said. "Cynthia said it was okay. We just need a place to practice."

"I ain't in no mood . . ." Vernon began to complain.

"There's nothing for you to do," I explained. "Just keep pumping that iron. We'll stay out of your way."

Before Vernon could complain anymore, we walked into the room and started setting up. He turned his back to us and kept lifting weights. Fifteen minutes later, we were ready to get under way. By then Vernon had lifted himself onto his cart and wheeled himself into the bathroom and shut the door.

"Okay, boys," I said. "Let's see if we can do a version of that song they've been playing on the radio. Folks seem to like it. Let's see . . . goes something like . . ."

I started singing "Crazy Love Is Good Love," the current Bambi Love hit. The band followed along and soon it all fell into place. We ran it down several times before the bathroom door opened and Vernon came out, pushing his cart until he was right next to me.

"That's my song," he said. "That's 'Wild Country Night.'"

"No, sir. Bambi Love's singing it on the radio and saying she wrote it with her producer, Slick Walters. She says it's 'Crazy Love Is Good Love.'"

"Marla," said Vernon. "That's Marla doing nothing but switching up the lyrics. The original lyrics made sense. These don't."

"How'd the original lyrics go?" I asked.

Despite himself, Vernon started singing:

Peaceful afternoon
Sunny and bright
Then the day gives way
To a wild country night
Everyone'll be dancing
Till we all reach the heights
And have ourselves a ball
On this wild country night

God bless my band, 'cause the second Vernon hit his first note, we were right there behind him, as if we'd been his backup for years. I know he was amazed. I know he was moved. I know, because he didn't stop singing, he sang the song three, four, five times in a row. Each time he—and we—sounded better. Each time he grew more animated, bending the notes and gesturing with his hands. It was a feel-good, kick-ass party song, making all of us feel great.

"Helluva tune you wrote there," I said. "Now what

about this one Bambi calls 'Something I Got'? You heard this?"

Without waiting for Vernon's answer, I broke into Bambi's version:

You were living your life with nothing to do
Till everything changed when I came through
I got your attention, whether you liked it or not
'Cause, baby, it's all about that something I got
Something I got, I didn't learn in no school
Something I got, made you my fool
Something I got, and it ain't no shame
Something I got, got you calling my name

"Where'd you hear that?" asked Vernon.

"On the radio," I said. "Don't you ever listen to the radio?"

"Never. And Marla was singing it?"

"Calling herself 'Bambi' and telling the world she wrote it."

"She stole it."

"Let's hear the original she stole it from."

Without hesitating, Vernon launched into his version. After the first chorus, me and the band found the right notes and came in to back him up.

I was a lonely soul with nothing to do
But everything changed the day I met you
You grabbed my attention, and cold turned
to hot
All 'cause of that certain something you got
Something you got, they don't teach it in school
Something you got, made me break all the rules
Something you got, has me down on my knees
Something you got, got me pleading, please
please please

He sang so forcefully, so passionately, so sincerely that me and my musicians couldn't help but respond to his performance with hoots and hollers.

Hearing the reaction, Vernon had to smile.

"Marla sang it on the record," he said.

"I know," I said, "but she didn't sing it like that."

"I wasn't into singing then."

"You sang 'Faith,'" I reminded him. "You sang it beautifully. You made it a hit. Wanna try to sing it now?"

Before he could answer, I played the first notes on my guitar. That got him to singing . . .

Thank you for your faith
I'm not sure I deserve it

Thank you for your faith
I'm not sure I've preserved it
I know it's a gift
I can feel it pure and true
Thank you for your faith—
I'll always have faith in you

I could see Vernon choking back tears. I wanted to tell him to let go, to let the tears flow, but I knew the best thing I could do was shut up and keep playing.

"How 'bout 'Dreamin' in Blue'?"

"Man," said Vernon, "you really know my stuff."

"Been listening to it," I said. "Been liking it."

"Marla sang 'Dreamin' in Blue.' She nailed it. Is this another one she's copied?"

"You guessed it. She calls it 'Dreamin' of You.'"

"So what in hell did she and her producer do—steal every last song of mine?"

"Something like that," I said. "But don't think about that now. Just see if you can remember the original."

Vernon began singing, and it didn't take long for us to chime in with the right musical accompaniment.

Spent my days looking for you
Then spent my nights dreamin' in blue

Dreamin' you'd come back, faithful and true
So I could stop cryin' and dreamin' in blue
Dreamin' of happiness and a life brand-new
Guess I'll just go on dreamin' in blue

I also explained to Vernon how his "Cheatin' Days" had been changed into "Cheatin' Ways."

He just shook his head in wonder and dismay before breaking into the original version. Because I'd listened to his records so many times—and made my band listen as well—I knew all Vernon's songs. Like most songwriters, he hadn't forgotten a note or lyric of what he'd written. Going from one tune to another—from his "Cheatin' Days" and "Leaving Ain't the Last Thing on My Mind"—we barely gave him time to catch his breath. He even agreed to special requests—Skeeter's "Easygoing," a song he sang with relaxed charm and a big smile on his face. I wondered if, by asking him to sing "Surprising Love," a song he wrote with Jill, I would be pushing him too far. I decided not to ask him, but much to my delight, he sang it of his own volition.

I could see that, whatever attitude he tried to cling to when we'd begun, now he was transported. Now he was in another place altogether, a place where the music—*his* music—took hold of him and had him energized and I'd even say happy. Yes, for the first time ever, I saw that Vernon Clay, singing these songs in a voice filled with power and purpose, was a happy man.

Two hours after we started, I asked him, "How you feeling, man?"

"Not bad. But what happens now?"

"That's up to you."

THE LONGHORN BALLROOM

I got a funny story about Dewey Groom, the owner of the Longhorn Ballroom over in Dallas. This also happened in the strictly segregated 1960s. Just 'cause he was so great, I had Charley Pride, the then unknown black country singer, get onstage with me. When Dewey saw what I'd done, he went nuts. To add to the fun, I responded by kissing Charley full on the mouth. Naturally that enraged Dewey even more. But once Charley started singing, the beauty of his voice quickly calmed Dewey down.

In somewhat similar fashion, I knew Dewey wouldn't take well to the news that my band would be featuring a singer who'd be singing from a wheelchair.

It was two weeks before Christmas, when the club was always crowded.

"It's a time," said Dewey, "when folks wanna dance. Seeing some guy in a wheelchair don't make nobody wanna dance."

"Half of 'em are too drunk to notice who's singing," I said.

"I don't like the idea."

"I do. It's my band, and I'm doing it."

Except I didn't. I didn't, 'cause Vernon flat-out refused to come out of the house when we went by to get him.

By then we had spent three afternoons in the pool house, three long rehearsals where we'd damn well nailed down arrangements to a dozen songs of Vernon's that he could sing the hell out of. At the last rehearsal, when I mentioned the idea of his performing with us at the Longhorn, he said he'd think about it. Given how powerfully he'd been singing, I took that as a yes.

"He says no," Cynthia told us when we arrived at the house the night of the gig.

"I'll go back and talk to him," I said. "I even brought a wheelchair to make it easier for him."

"He asked that you not go back there. He asked that you respect his privacy."

"What do you think is going on with him, Cynthia?"

"A lot. I think you woke up something inside him that's been asleep for a long time."

"But it's a positive thing," I said. "His creative juices are flowing again."

"Flowing so strong they might even be a little scary."

"You don't think it'd do him good to play in front of people?"

"This isn't about what I think," said Cynthia, "it's what Vernon thinks. I don't have to tell you—he's been through hell. For a long time he's been hiding from his feelings. His music is beautiful, but his music brings back all those feelings. And now, learning how he's been swindled, he has a whole bunch of new feelings to contend with."

I saw Cynthia's point. I knew she was right. At the same time, I had my heart set on seeing him sing in front of a crowd. I was sure the crowd would love him, and that love would make him feel great. Or at least make me feel great. On second thought, maybe I was thinking more about myself than him. It wasn't about making *me* feel good, it was about making *Vernon* feel good. And if Cynthia was right, as I suspected she was, right now he wasn't feeling good at all. He was feeling confused. Best to leave him alone.

We went on and played the Longhorn that night and the night after. The crowd was large and enthusiastic. I played my best, but my mind was elsewhere. I couldn't stop thinking about Vernon and how this same crowd would react to him. In my gut, I just knew it'd be good for him to get the recognition he deserved.

"Where's your wheelchair singer?" asked Dewey Groom. After all his objections, he sounded halfway disappointed.

"He's under the weather. Another time."

"I see where that singer—the one you said stole his songs—is coming to Fort Worth."

"What are you talking about?"

"Bambi Love. Isn't she the one?"

"What about Bambi Love?"

"Something about her doing a special Christmas Eve concert at Leonards department store."

"What!"

"From what I hear, Nutsy Perkins is promoting the whole thing. He got old man J. M. Leonard to turn part of the store into a stage. Right back there by the toy department. It's gonna be a huge event."

"I don't believe it," I said.

"You don't have to, but from what I understand, Nutsy once did Leonard a solid, and now Leonard's paying him back."

That just didn't compute. Nutsy Perkins wasn't a music promoter. He probably never even heard of Bambi Love till I told him the story. Of course Ranger Roy Finkelstein, who ran the Record Dump, knew how popular she was. Was Ranger Roy behind the whole thing? But why would he encourage Nutsy to do this? A quick way to make a buck? A way to spite me? It made no sense. I didn't get it. Something wasn't right.

In all probability, Dewey got it wrong. Dewey, who liked his liquor, wasn't always the most reliable source of accurate information.

The more I thought about it, the more I knew it couldn't be true.

THE STORY BEHIND THE STORY

I ripped the poster off the telephone pole, put it in my car and made the drive from Fort Worth to Dallas in record time. I was going to see Vernon.

The poster, in Christmas colors of green and red, had large screaming letters that said:

ONE NIGHT ONLY!

CHRISTMAS EVE!

AMERICA'S NEWEST SWEETHEART

MISS BAMBI LOVE

LEONARDS DEPARTMENT STORE

SECOND FLOOR

By the time I arrived at the home of Cynthia and Ryan Smith, I had all my arguments lined up.

"He still doesn't want to see you," said Cynthia.

"Has he seen this?" I asked, showing her the poster.

She read it quickly and said, "I don't think so."

"They've also been advertising it on the radio," I said.

"Vernon doesn't listen to the radio."

"I think he needs to listen to me. I really do."

"I don't see how hearing about this is gonna make him feel any better."

"I do," I said.

"How?"

"I want him there," I said with so much conviction I even surprised myself.

"He'll never do it. He doesn't want to see her. What's the point?"

"I think I can make him see the point. I just need to talk to him."

Cynthia hesitated for several seconds. She still wasn't convinced.

"You know me well enough to see that I mean the guy no harm," I said. "I've been on a long mission to help him."

"And you want the mission to end with him being hurt?"

"That's not want I want."

"Well, what *do* you want, Willie?" she asked me. "I know this is some pet project of yours. But as far as I can see, all you're doing is opening old wounds, wounds causing him terrible pain."

"He's had enough pain, I agree."

"Then why cause him more?"

"I'm not."

"I don't understand what you're really up to. I don't see your plan."

"I can't explain it now, but if you let me go back and talk to him, I can make him understand."

More silence, more hesitation on Cynthia's part. She closed her eyes. She sighed. She opened her eyes and said, "Look, he's an adult. He can make up his own mind. Go back there, knock on the door, but I can't guarantee he'll let you in, or if he does, if he'll even listen to you."

I went back.

I knocked on the door.

He answered.

I usually don't like confrontations. I avoid them whenever I can. Don't like folks getting in my face, and I don't like getting in theirs. Most confrontations don't accomplish a damn thing. All they do is promote more bad feelings.

I knew better than to confront Vernon.

"I've been thinking about you, buddy," was all I said.

"You been thinking about me too much."

"You're probably right."

"Then stop."

"I will."

"I don't wanna be anybody's cause," he said. "Don't wanna be anybody's charity case."

"I understand."

"Do you really?"

"Yes indeed," I assured him.

"Then what the hell are you doing here?" he asked.

"I'm here to discuss something else entirely."

"What?"

"Chili rice."

★ FORT WORTH STAR-TELEGRAM ★

RECORD PRODUCER ACCUSED OF THEFT

On the morning before this evening's much-anticipated concert at Leonards department store, singer Bambi Love and her manager, Jack "Slick" Walters, were slapped with a copyright violation lawsuit alleging that eight songs released by Love and purportedly written by Love and Walters are, in fact, near carbon copies of compositions penned by Love's former band leader, Vernon Clay.

Attorney Norby B. Green, who successfully defended Nathan "Nutsy" Perkins against charges of grand larceny in a celebrated case earlier this year, filed the papers on behalf of Mr. Clay.

"This is an instance where the thievery is as audacious as it obvious," said Green. "What makes the illegality especially grievous is that it occurred not simply once, but eight separate times. I see this as an open-

and-shut case. If it goes to trial, which I rather doubt, I expect justice to be rendered quickly. The guilty parties will pay, and pay dearly."

The lawsuit cites damages and asks that the copyrights be reassigned to Clay and asks for damages of $100,000.

After being served papers, the singer and producer had no comment before leaving Fort Worth and canceling Love's appearance at Leonards tonight.

A spokesman for Leonards, however, did say that the Christmas Eve concert would go on as scheduled, with several surprise guests.

CHRISTMAS EVE

I'm writing this with green ink on bright red paper. I'm writing it so that, no matter what happens to me, I'll have this memory. I'm writing it so I can come back and relive it whenever I want to. I'm writing down every detail I can remember so that evening, the best of my life, will live forever.

I'd always seen the Christmas season as the worst time of the year. It was a time that I dreaded, a time when I lost my parents, my grandmother, Jill and Vicky. I never thought I'd live to see Christmas as anything but a dark season of death.

So how could my attitude ever change? How could I ever come to love a season I had so long hated?

Let me explain. Let me start out by remembering the super-strong aroma of chili rice.

When I was told that Chester and Essie had been hired to make big vats of Grandma's recipe, enough to feed an army of Christmas shoppers, I knew it was time to drop my resistance and go with the flow of the good things coming my way.

Strange as it may seem, I'd never been inside Leonards. All those months of hawking my pretty paper outside the store, and yet not once did I venture in. Maybe it's 'cause I didn't feel I belonged, or maybe 'cause I was scared I'd be kicked out or stepped over. The reasons don't matter now, 'cause it felt extra special to roll myself through those front doors in a wheelchair that had my name in glitter letters written across the back. Still nervous, still unsure of what would happen, I expected to face strangers, but instead I was greeted by Chester and Essie—who gave me big smiles and big hugs—and right off thanked me for getting them the biggest catering gig of their life. I tried to explain that it wasn't me, it was my friends, but Essie wasn't having it, all Essie could say was "It's all you. Look at all the good you done!"

The first floor of Leonards was decked out with hundreds of white streamers that shimmered like icicles. Huge lacy cutouts in the shape of snowflakes dangled down from the ceiling. Excited customers shared the aisles with four separate roving groups of Christmas carolers singing "God Rest Ye Merry, Gentlemen," "Silent Night," "Deck the Halls" and "O Come, All Ye Faithful."

The elevator, decorated with candy canes and mistletoe, opened to the second floor, where a thirty-foot giant Christmas tree was aglow with a thousand silver fairies and princesses and a glistening golden star on top.

I followed my friends.

They were all there—Cynthia and Ryan and even Cynthia's parents, Virginia and Reggie. Willie was there, and so was Brother Paul and the rest of the band, along with the lawyer I'd just met yesterday, Norby Green. Nutsy Perkins and Ranger Roy Finkelstein, the guys who introduced me to Norby, were there to cheer me on and join the swelling crowd of well-wishers accompanying me to the stage built in the middle of the toy department, right next to Santa's workshop with its dozens of elf and reindeer dolls.

There came Santa himself, riding in on a special monorail Leonards had set up for the Christmas season. Underneath the red suit and beard, I saw it was Big Bill from Big Bill's bar. So it was shiny-nosed Santa Bill who pushed me onstage and set me in front of the microphone. In his booming voice, Santa Bill said, "Ladies and gentlemen, you didn't know it, but this is the gift you've been waiting for. This is the best gift you're gonna get this Christmas—or any Christmas to come. This is a very special, very talented, very great singer and songwriter. So say 'Merry Christmas' to Mr. Vernon Clay!"

The crowd shouted out "Merry Christmas, Vernon!" and bells started ringing and chimes started chiming and Willie, wearing a silly Santa cap and smiling that sly smile of his, kicked off "Faith" and I sang it, with tears streaming down my cheeks, wishing only that my grandmother were there to see everything I was seeing and feel everything I was feeling. Because as I kept singing the songs that were born out of my soul—"Wild Country Night" and "Dreamin' in Blue" and "Something You Got" and "Leaving Ain't the Last Thing on My Mind" and all the others—I knew I wouldn't be there except for that woman's devotion. The music I've made, the tunes I've written, the trips I've taken, the story I've written out on this pretty paper, even the two women I've loved—none of it would be possible if I hadn't been loved by a grandmother who, just by being herself, taught me love.

It's love that I was feeling on that Christmas Eve, love that I was singing 'bout in all my songs, love that was flying up there in my direction and smacking me in the face, love from all the folks stomping and shouting and calling out my name—"Vernon! Vernon! Vernon!"

Yet even in the midst of so much beautiful excitement and beautiful music, even being surrounded by the holiday joy and heartfelt prayers for peace on earth and goodwill toward men, underneath it all I could still sense the soul of the littlest angel who wasn't there that night except in spirit. And I heard her spirit, I heard her voice, I heard her singing as she will always sing, sweetly and softly . . .

Rain rain go away
Come back another day
Little Vicky wants to play
So please make everything okay

ACKNOWLEDGMENTS

David Ritz would like to thank Willie, for all the faith and trust; Mark Rothbaum, for coming up with the idea; David Rosenthal, for believing; Brant Rumble, for superb guidance; and David Vigliano, for steely strong support.

Love to all my family and friends. And special thanks to Roberta, for her insightful editorial suggestions.